The Hidden Window Mystery

Books by

CAROLYN KEENE

Nancy Drew Mystery Stories

Dana Girls Mystery Stories

Without warning, a trap door in the floor opened

NANCY DREW MYSTERY STORIES

The Hidden Window Mystery

BY CAROLYN KEENE

NEW YORK

Grosset & Dunlap

PUBLISHERS

PRINTED IN THE UNITED STATES OF AMERICA

Contents

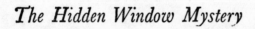

The Hidden Window Mystery

CHAPTER I

The Peacock Mystery

"GOOD-BY, Hannah!" said Nancy Drew. She gave the housekeeper a hug, then put a hand on the front-door knob.

"Watch out for falling tree branches," Hannah Gruen warned the attractive blond girl. "This is the most terrific April wind I've ever seen."

Outside, there was continuous roar. But above it, both Nancy and Mrs. Gruen suddenly heard a loud crash on the front porch.

"What was that?" the motherly looking housekeeper asked worriedly.

Nancy yanked the door open. "Oh!" she exclaimed.

Lying in a heap near the edge of the porch was the mailman, Mr. Ritter. He was unconscious. His bag had tumbled down the steps and letters and magazines were flying about.

Nancy and Mrs. Gruen rushed to the man's

side. He evidently had hit his head, for there was a large red mark on his temple. They lifted the victim gently and carried him into the living room.

"Maybe we'd better call a doctor," Nancy suggested.

At that moment Mr. Ritter's eyelids flickered. In a moment the sixty-year-old postman regained consciousness and refused to have a doctor.

"I'll be all right in a minute, but I'd appreciate it if you'd bring in my mailbag. And by the way, there's something in it you'll be mighty interested in."

Nancy hurried from the house. Her blue eyes sparkling in anticipation, she began to gather up the letters, newspapers, and magazines that were being swirled across the neighboring lawns by the strong winds. It took Nancy nearly ten minutes to collect the mail.

Entering the living room with the mailbag slung over her shoulder, she was glad to see Mr. Ritter sitting up in a chair and drinking a cup of tea.

"Oh, thank you, Nancy," he said. "It was mighty careless of me to stumble and knock myself out. That wind is fierce. It blew some dirt into my eye and for a moment I couldn't see where I was going."

"How do you feel?" Nancy asked gently.

Mr. Ritter declared he would be ready to resume his deliveries in a few minutes. "I'd like to rest just a bit longer."

"May I help you sort the mail?" Nancy offered. "And what was it you wanted to show me?"

As Mr. Ritter began rummaging in the bag, he said, "I read an article in a magazine telling about a large reward. It's being offered to anyone who can solve the mystery of a missing stained-glass window."

Nancy was intrigued at once. "What magazine was the article in?" she asked eagerly.

Mr. Ritter pulled a torn, soiled copy of the *Continental* from his bag. "Here's a copy of the same magazine. It's for your new neighbor Mrs. Dondo."

Nancy said she did not know the woman.

"I'm sure she won't mind if you look at the article," the postman said. "You're a good amateur detective, Nancy, but if you can solve this one, you'll certainly put another feather in your cap."

Nancy smiled and began to read. Sir Richard Greystone of England was trying to trace a medieval stained-glass window which had been in his family since the fourteenth century. He believed that the window had been brought to the United States about 1850 but all trace of it had been lost. Sir Richard was offering a large reward for any information leading to its whereabouts.

The article went on to describe the window which pictured a knight riding off to battle. The family shield he was holding had a peacock emblazoned on it.

Nancy's eyes danced with excitement. "Thank you, Mr. Ritter, for telling me about this," she said. "I'll read it to you, Hannah."

The housekeeper smiled. "I was hoping you would. By the way, that's a mighty good-looking foreign car pictured on the back."

Nancy turned the magazine over and looked at the advertisement. The car, though small in size, was of sleek design and could travel over a hundred miles an hour.

Turning again to the article, Nancy read it aloud. Hannah paled a bit. "A peacock on the shield, eh?" she said. "You know some folks think peacocks, especially the feathers in their fan tails, bring bad luck."

"But I know you don't believe that," Nancy remarked.

"Those marks in the fan," the housekeeper stated, "are said to be evil eyes." She looked at Nancy affectionately. "But I always taught you not to be superstitious."

Hannah Gruen had lived with the Drews and taken care of Nancy ever since the girl's mother had passed away fifteen years ago when Nancy was three years old.

Nancy remarked that in India peacocks are held to be sacred.

"That's right," Mr. Ritter spoke up. "And so are the cow and the monkey."

The postman stood up and declared that he felt well enough to resume his delivery route. "I'm already late," he said. "Folks will be wondering what's happened to their mail."

He thanked Nancy and Hannah for their assistance, then started for the door, accompanied by the others. As he reached it, the bell rang and someone began pounding loudly on the door.

When Mr. Ritter opened it, Nancy and Hannah saw a strange woman standing there. Her bleached blond hair, blown by the wind, stuck out straight from her head. She was short and sallow-complexioned. Her dark eyes blazed.

"How do you do, Mrs. Dondo?" said Mr. Ritter.

The woman did not acknowledge the greeting, and ignored Nancy and Hannah. Waving a fist at the postman, she said:

"I saw what was going on. You're the most careless mailman I've ever known! I saw you taking time out here. Why aren't you on the job?"

Nancy and the others were so startled by the woman's irate manner that they stood open-mouthed.

"Listen here, Mr. Ritter," the woman went on,

"you've got some mail for me and I want it right away.   There's an important letter I have to have and you've been dillydallying all this time.   Give it to me at once!"

Mrs. Dondo pushed into the hall and leaned over the mailbag.   She put her hand in to grab a letter, but Mr. Ritter told her he would tend to this himself.   Quickly he went over every letter in the pouch.

"There's no mail for you today, Mrs. Dondo, except a magazine," he said.   He handed the *Continental* to her.

"And what a mess it is!" she shouted.   "More of your carelessness.   And don't tell me there wasn't a letter for me.   It was in your bag before you let the mail blow all over the neighborhood. You'd better find it too!   That letter had a hundred dollars in it and I don't propose to lose it!"

"A hundred dollars!" Mr. Ritter cried out, a look of alarm coming over his face.

"Yes, a hundred dollars!" Mrs. Dondo repeated. "And if you've lost that letter, you're going to pay me the money yourself!"

CHAPTER II

An Unpleasant Neighbor

FOR a moment Nancy thought Mr. Ritter was going to collapse again—he was so upset. "Mrs. Dondo," she asked, "do you have any proof that the letter was in this particular delivery?"

"You keep out of this," the woman said, glaring at Nancy. "I'll handle the matter in my own way."

"I doubt that you could make any claim," the young sleuth went on, despite the rebuff.

"I'll get proof and I'll see that I get paid!" Mrs. Dondo screamed. "I'll carry this story to the postmaster!"

Hannah Gruen stepped forward. "But right now you'll get out of this house," she said firmly. With an angry shrug the unpleasant woman turned and left. Nancy asked Mr. Ritter where she lived.

"Down near the corner," he replied.

Nancy offered to make a further search for Mrs. Dondo's letter or any others which she might have missed. From the time that Nancy had discovered *The Secret of the Old Clock,* up to the young detective's latest adventure, *The Witch Tree Symbol,* she had been helping people, often involving herself in grave danger.

"My little terrier, Togo, is good at finding things," Nancy told the postman. "I'll get him to help me."

She urged Mr. Ritter not to be too concerned about Mrs. Dondo's accusation, but the postman said he was worried. Even though the woman might not be able to collect the money from him, a complaint to the postmaster for carelessness would be a black mark on his record.

"And I'm near retirement age," he added. "I've been bringing you letters since you were knee-high to a grasshopper, Nancy."

"Yes, I know," she said, smiling at him affectionately.

After Mr. Ritter had gone, Nancy hurried to the kitchen where Togo was taking a nap. "Before I go shopping, old fellow," she said, "we have a job to do. Come with me."

The little dog jumped up, cocked his head, and followed his mistress into the front hall. She was showing him a white envelope when the telephone rang. The caller was Bess Marvin, one of Nancy's two best friends.

"What's new?" Bess asked.

"A couple of mysteries. Why don't you and George come over and I'll tell you all about them?"

"Sounds like fun. We'll be right there."

George Fayne and Bess Marvin were cousins. George, in keeping with her boyish name, wore her dark hair short and preferred tailored clothes. Bess, in contrast, was very feminine and wore frilly dresses. She was blond and slightly overweight because of her fondness for rich food.

Nancy went outside to wait for the girls who arrived in exactly ten minutes.

"Hypers, Nancy," said George, "you hardly give us time to recover from one mystery before you have another to solve. What's going on now?"

Nancy laughed. Then, sobering, she quickly explained the necessity of a further hunt for Mrs. Dondo's letter.

When she finished, Bess said, "I've heard Mother speak of Mrs. Dondo. She says the woman is a troublemaker."

George warned, "You'd better be careful, Nancy."

"In what way is she a troublemaker?" Nancy asked.

Bess said that Mrs. Dondo had come from Virginia. "She left there because of some unpleasantness with her neighbors, Mother said. At least, that's what Mother heard at a club meeting."

"What was the matter with her?" George demanded.

Bess said Mrs. Dondo was a social climber and a schemer, a very ordinary person. "She isn't a bit like other people in this neighborhood," Bess went on. "I can't understand why she came here."

Meanwhile, Togo had been crawling under the hedges and foundation plantings of nearby homes looking for envelopes like the one his mistress had shown him. Nancy herself, while waiting for the girls, had been looking in the trees and high bushes. Neither she nor the dog had had any luck.

Bess and George eagerly joined in the search and for nearly half an hour the group combed the entire area thoroughly.

Finally Bess sighed. "If there were ever any letters around here, they're gone now. Maybe other neighbors found them."

"That's very possible," Nancy agreed. She said that since all the families in the neighborhood were fine people, they certainly would have delivered any mail they found to the addressees.

"Then maybe Mrs. Dondo has her letter by now," George suggested. "Let's go find out."

"And if she doesn't," said Nancy, "I'm going to try talking her out of going to the postmaster. I'd hate to see Mr. Ritter get into trouble. He's such a darling."

The three girls walked to the Dondo house. Before they had a chance to ring the bell, sounds of quarreling voices came from an open window. A man, whom the girls assumed to be Mr. Dondo, was reprimanding his wife.

"That was a pretty cheap trick of yours, trying to get easy money out of the postman."

The woman flared in reply. "What do you know about it?"

"I know this much," the man replied. "That good-for-nothing brother of yours, Alonzo, would never send you a hundred dollars."

"Oh, be quiet!" Mrs. Dondo screamed. "Alonzo is all right. You just don't like him."

"You bet I don't like him, and for good reason, too. Alonzo's too slick for his own good. If he ever told you he was sending you a hundred dollars, he sure was kidding you."

When Mrs. Dondo would not admit that her husband was right, he said, "I don't like your brother's business dealings, but I don't think he's stupid. Alonzo would never send that much money in cash through the mail."

The three girls looked at one another and smiled. Nancy had never picked up such incriminating information just by accidental eavesdropping! She and her friends tiptoed away and hurried back with Togo to Nancy's house.

"Mrs. Dondo still may try to make trouble for Mr. Ritter," said Bess, as they went inside.

"Let her try it!" George said with disgust. "Nancy, Bess told me that you had two cases to solve. What's the other one?"

Nancy smiled. "The three of us are going to hunt for a stained-glass window."

"What!" the cousins chorused.

Quickly Nancy explained about the article in the *Continental* and the reward being offered to anyone finding the old window that pictured the knight with the peacock shield.

George looked interested, then grinned. With a twinkle in her eye, she asked, "Nancy, what'll you do with all that money? You may ruin your amateur standing as a detective."

Nancy quickly explained that she would not take the money for herself. "I've been thinking I'd love to make a sizable donation to the Hospital Fund—toward the new children's wing. If I won the reward money, it could be paid directly to the hospital."

"That sounds wonderful," said Bess.

"Will you help me?" Nancy asked the cousins. "Then we can make the donation together."

George agreed at once, but Bess said there was one angle to the mystery which worried her. She was seated in a large upholstered chair in the living room, near the doorway into the hall. Now she pulled her feet up under her and propped her chin on one fist. "I don't like this peacock business."

"Don't tell me you're superstitious about pea-cocks!" George said in amusement.

Bess turned to Nancy and asked, "Have you any theory as to what happened to the stained-glass window?"

"No," the young sleuth replied. "Of course the window may have been destroyed long ago, but I'm hoping it hasn't been."

"It could have been taken down and stored away," George said. "People sometimes get tired of looking at stained-glass windows and remove them, just as they do pictures."

"The place where the window was may have changed owners several times," Bess said. "They probably had a lot of hard luck and blamed it on those evil eyes in the peacock's fan."

"Oh, Bess," said George, "you always—"

The words were hardly spoken when a terrific bang startled Nancy and her friends.

The next moment a gust of wind rushed into the room, carrying with it a large peacock feather which came to rest at Bess's feet! The girl shrieked.

CHAPTER III

A Plea for Help

FOR a few tense seconds the girls did not move. Bess was too terrified, George and Nancy too startled.

Then Nancy sprang from her chair and dashed into the hall. Wind roared through the wide-open front door. As Nancy slammed it shut, she looked around, trying to figure out where the peacock feather had come from.

Gazing up the stairway, she exclaimed, "Hannah!" Mrs. Gruen was coming down the steps, a bunch of peacock feathers in one hand!

By this time Bess and George had also reached the hall. They looked at the housekeeper in amazement, then Bess said:

"You scared the wits out of me, Hannah! And—and who opened the front door?"

"I'm sure it was only the wind," Nancy replied. "Who was the last to come in?"

Bess sheepishly admitted that she had been.

14

Probably she had not closed the door tightly. Then she turned to Mrs. Gruen, who by this time had reached the first floor.

"Where did you find those?" Bess asked her, eying the bunch of feathers.

The housekeeper explained. "After talking with Nancy about the peacock and that stained-glass window, I remembered these feathers. They've been in the attic for years. They belonged to Nancy's grandmother, Mrs. Austin."

Hannah Gruen laid the peacock feathers on a table in the living room and the girls examined them closely.

"Aren't they beautiful?" Nancy remarked. "I understand the formation of the eyes in the feathers is one of the most unusual things in nature."

"Indeed it is," said Hannah, "and the bird is very proud of his feathers. Remember that old expression 'vain as a peacock'?"

When the girls nodded, Hannah continued, "It comes from the fact that a peacock greatly values his fan. It's said that when his tail feathers are plucked to be sold, the bird is so ashamed he hides for days. He won't eat and sometimes mourns his loss until he dies of starvation."

"Oh, how awful!" Bess remarked.

Just then the girls heard a key in the front door. A moment later Mr. Drew let himself into the house. A tall and handsome man, Nancy's father practiced law in River Heights.

"Hi, Dad!" Nancy said, hurrying to kiss him.

He greeted the others, then asked Nancy teasingly, "Do I detect a gleam in those blue eyes that means you're involved in another mystery?"

Smiling, Nancy nodded as she hung up his coat. Then she told her father about Mr. Ritter's accident and Mrs. Dondo's accusation.

"That's too bad," the lawyer commented as the group walked into the living room.

When Mr. Drew had settled in his favorite chair, Nancy told him the story of the missing stained-glass window.

"That's very interesting," said Mr. Drew when she finished, "but tracing a window lost since 1850 will require considerable investigation."

"But it'll be fun," said Nancy, then asked if he had any suggestions on how she might proceed.

The lawyer thought for a moment, then said that he had a client named Mr. Atwater who was an authority on stained-glass windows. The man had formerly owned a large studio in a nearby town where he had made windows for churches and other buildings.

"Perhaps you'd like to talk with him, Nancy."

"I'd love to. Where does Mr. Atwater live?"

"Five miles from River Heights," Mr. Drew replied. "He's retired now and not in the best of health, but he loves to talk about his art. Perhaps I can make an appointment for you to see him tomorrow. It's Saturday and he may not be busy."

"I'd like to go along," George spoke up.

"Me too," Bess added. "Does your friend still make stained-glass windows, Mr. Drew?"

"Yes, but only as a hobby. He has a very complete studio at his home."

Mr. Drew went to the telephone. A few minutes later he returned to say that the elderly artist would be delighted to see the girls at ten o'clock the next morning.

At twenty minutes to ten the following day Nancy picked up Bess and George in her convertible. Since the wind had stopped blowing and it was a beautiful day, Nancy had put the top down.

The drive to Mr. Atwater's home took only fifteen minutes. Nancy parked her car in the rear of the property near a building which she thought must be the studio. A tall, slender man with white hair came out of the building and walked toward the girls.

"How do you do," said Nancy, smiling. "Are you Mr. Atwater?"

"I certainly am," replied the man. Despite his height, he was frail in appearance. "You're right on time, Miss Drew. I recognized you from the picture I've often seen on your dad's desk."

Nancy introduced her friends. "Glad to meet

you, girls," the artist said, and led the way inside his one-room studio.

The place was extremely neat. Rows of tools hung above an immaculate workbench. A drawing table and a cutting bench were arranged along one wall, and in a far corner stood a stove.

Mr. Atwater invited the girls to sit down in easy chairs. "Your father mentioned some mystery in connection with your visit here," he said to Nancy.

"Yes, there is one I'd like to solve." She asked him if he had heard about the window which Sir Richard Greystone was eager to find. When Mr. Atwater shook his head, Nancy told him of the article in *Continental* and the reward.

The artist smiled. "I wish I were well enough to try to find the missing window," he said. "But I'll do everything I can to help you locate it."

Nancy thanked him and said, "I presume that if the window is still in existence, its colors are very lovely. I understand that modern stained-glass windows don't have the same striking effect as those of the middle ages."

Mr. Atwater nodded. "That is true. The old-time glass had many imperfections—for example, there were bubbles in it. But these very weaknesses have given the windows their lovely satiny appearance."

"How are modern stained-glass windows made?" George spoke up.

"Well," said Mr. Atwater, "I'll try to give you a brief description. First, I would take measurements and ascertain the direction and amount of light which would fall on the window in its future setting."

"Is that so you would know how much depth of color to use?" Nancy asked.

"Exactly!" Mr. Atwater said. "Next, I'd make a small-sized sketch of the picture. Then I would color it—"

"And I'd approve it, I'm sure!" George interrupted with a chuckle, looking around at some lovely window sketches on the studio walls.

Mr. Atwater smiled. "If so, the sketch would be enlarged into a working drawing, called a cartoon. Then it would be marked up to show the actual size and shape of each piece of glass and what colors they were to be.

"Next, transparent paper would be laid over the drawing and the design copied exactly. Then I'd cut this paper along the dividing lines and I'd have a pattern for each piece of glass to be cut."

"When do you cut the glass?" Bess questioned.

"That's the next step. I lay the pieces of the pattern on sheets of glass in the colors I want and cut them out. When they're ready, I assemble my colored glass picture onto a large plain sheet of glass and fasten it down with molten beeswax."

He glanced at a saucepan on top of the stove. "I was just melting some before you came.

"My picture," Mr. Atwater said, "is now fitted into a frame, and black lines, representing the leading between the pieces of glass, are painted on. Then, by holding the picture up to the light, I can get the over-all effect of color and design before adding the details of the picture which I paint in by hand."

"My," said Bess, "it certainly *is* complicated."

"Yes," agreed Nancy. "I had no idea there were so many steps in making stained-glass windows."

Mr. Atwater smiled. "There are several more. Next comes the leading."

Nancy noticed that the elderly man's kind face showed signs of weariness. "I'm afraid," she said gently, "we've been so interested that we didn't realize how much time has passed. Perhaps we can come back again."

The man admitted he was tired, but urged the girls to pay him another visit soon. They thanked Mr. Atwater for the invitation and got up to leave.

As George went toward the door, one foot suddenly skidded on the floor. In trying to keep her balance, she clutched wildly at a table on which there was a sharp piece of plate glass.

"Oh!" she exclaimed, as blood spurted from a deep cut on the palm of her right hand.

Mr. Atwater sprang to George's side. "I'm

dreadfully sorry," he said. "It's my fault. I must have spilled some beeswax on the floor."

The artist hurried to a first-aid kit hanging on one wall and opened it. After thoroughly cleansing the wound on George's hand, he deftly bandaged it. During the treatment he apologized profusely.

George was more concerned for Mr. Atwater than over her own mishap. He was so pale that she was afraid he might faint.

"It's nothing," she insisted. "The cut will soon heal."

Nancy, too, remembered what her father had said about the elderly man's health. "Perhaps you should rest now," she said kindly.

"I will," he promised, "but first let me give you a catalog. It contains a list of all the prominent firms and individuals who make stained-glass windows," he added, handing her the booklet.

"Thank you," said Nancy. "I'm sure it will be a great help in my search."

The three girls left Mr. Atwater at the back door of his house, then drove off to their homes. After lunch Nancy sat down to study the catalog. The list of names was long. She turned page after page. None yielded a clue which Nancy thought might lead to the missing window.

Just as the young sleuth reached the *W's* in the alphabetical list, Hannah Gruen came into the room. "Have you had any luck, Nancy?" she asked.

"Not until this very second," the girl replied. "Hannah, you brought it to me!"

"Whatever are you talking about?" the housekeeper asked, looking over Nancy's shoulder.

She followed the young detective's finger to a notation which read:

WAVERLY STUDIO
Mark Bradshaw, *Owner*
Charlottesville, Va.

"Charlottesville!" Nancy exclaimed. "That whole area was settled by English people. It's a perfect place to start looking for the Greystones' stained-glass window!"

"Do you think this Mr. Bradshaw might know something about it?" Hannah asked.

"I'm hoping so," Nancy replied. Then her face broke into a big smile. "What's more, Hannah, Charlottesville is where my cousin Susan Carr lives. She's often invited me and Bess and George to come see her!"

"It *would* be nice for you to visit Susan and her husband Cliff," Hannah agreed. "And this is certainly an ideal time to go. Garden Week will be held there soon."

"That's right," said Nancy. "I'll get in touch with Susan this minute."

She went to the telephone and put in the long-distance call. Susan herself answered. Hearing of Nancy's plan to visit Charlottesville, she said she would be delighted to have the girls stay with her.

"You'll just adore it, Nance. Our garden is perfectly beautiful now. It's going to be open to the public during Garden Week."

"How wonderful, Sue!" said Nancy. Then she told her cousin about the stained-glass-window mystery.

"Sounds as if you're coming to the right place to look for it," Susan agreed.

Before hanging up, Susan said she would give a party for the girls. She wanted them to meet the new friends that the Carrs had made during the two years they had lived in Virginia.

"So bring something dressy," she advised.

"We will," Nancy promised. "Good-by now."

She had just put down the phone when it rang. Nancy picked it up again and said hello.

"Nancy, this is Mr. Ritter." The postman's voice was strained. "Something terrible has happened. I need your help at once!"

CHAPTER IV

A Puzzling Telegram

"I'LL be glad to help you if I can," Nancy told
Mr. Ritter. "Is it something to do with Mrs.
Dondo?"

"Yes," the man replied. "When I went there
this morning, she showed me an air-mail, special-
delivery letter from her brother. He said he
had sent her a hundred-dollar bill which she
should have by now. Nancy, Mrs. Dondo is still
accusing me of stealing it and insists she is going
to take it up with the postal authorities and the
police!"

Nancy was alarmed. Even if Mrs. Dondo could
not prove her case, she could make it so unpleasant for Mr. Ritter that other people on his route
might lose confidence in him.

"I'll certainly do what I can for you," Nancy
told the postman. "Let's call on her right away,"
she suggested.

"I'll come right over to your house."

The postman arrived in a short time and together they walked to the Dondo home. The unpleasant woman opened the door herself.

"So you've brought your detective with you, I see," she said acidly. "Well, that's all right with me. Come in and I'll show her the letter from my brother."

Nancy stepped into the hall and followed the woman into her living room. The woman went to a desk, opened a drawer, and took out a letter which she handed to Nancy.

"Do you want me to read it?" Nancy asked.

"Yes. And I hope that will settle things once and for all."

Nancy glanced at the postmark and caught her breath. It was stamped Charlottesville, Virginia, the day before! In the left-hand corner was the sender's name—Alonzo Rugby. But there was no postbox number or street address.

The contents of the letter confirmed Mrs. Dondo's story. Short and to the point, it read:

> *Dear Sis,*
> *Like you asked me on the phone, I am writing this to tell you that I did send you a hundred-dollar bill in a letter a few days ago. You should have received it on Friday.*
> *Your loving brother,*
> *Alonzo*

Nancy glanced up. Mrs. Dondo was staring at her with narrowed eyes. Jaw set firmly, the woman said, "Now I guess you're convinced. But if you think I'm going to let Mr. Ritter get away with my hundred-dollar bill, you're very much mistaken."

Nancy returned Mrs. Dondo's stare. "I want to tell you something," she said. "I have known Mr. Ritter a long time. He is an honest man. It is most unfortunate that the letter was lost, but as I said yesterday, your brother never should have sent cash through the mail."

Mrs. Dondo's eyes flashed. "I don't want your advice, young lady!" Then her sallow face took on a cunning look as she said to Nancy, "Maybe you're right after all about Mr. Ritter not taking the money. You're the one who went around picking up the letters after he fell. I'm beginning to think you're the one who kept the money!"

Nancy was so furious at this accusation that for a few seconds she was tongue-tied. Then she said, "Mrs. Dondo, your statements are ridiculous and you know it. You haven't lived here long. But you'll find people in this neighborhood are friendly and honest. They're not suspicious of one another. I suggest that you drop this whole matter at once or you may find living here very unpleasant."

"That's right," Mr. Ritter spoke up. "And don't you dare accuse Nancy!"

Mrs. Dondo was taken aback for a moment but quickly recovered herself.

"I've got a good family too. My brother is a talented artist."

Then the scowl came back to her face. "Neighbors or no neighbors, I don't intend to be talked out of getting my hundred dollars back." She went to the front door and opened it. "Good-by," the woman said icily.

When Nancy reached the street with Mr. Ritter, she again urged the postman not to worry. "In any case, I'll tell my father about this latest development and he can take care of everything. Incidentally, I'm going away on a short trip, Mr. Ritter."

When she told him that her destination was Charlottesville and that she would look up Alonzo Rugby, Mr. Ritter smiled for the first time that afternoon. "You're a real friend, Nancy," he said. "Thanks a lot and ask your father to get in touch with me."

As soon as Nancy was inside her own house, she telephoned her father and gave him all the details. He promised to watch out for Mr. Ritter's interest should the need arise.

"Mrs. Dondo has a weak case," he said. "But she may try to start a whispering campaign around our neighborhood that could prove to be very unpleasant for you. I'll certainly do my best to stop her."

Nancy now sought out Hannah Gruen for advice as to what clothes she should take to Charlottesville, and told about the party Susan was going to give for the girls.

"Oh, do take that green linen with the rounded neckline," the housekeeper advised. "It looks so well on you. And besides," she added with a chuckle, "if you find that stained-glass peacock window, you'll want to celebrate in something that will match the bird's fan!"

Nancy smiled and went upstairs to assemble the green dress, a traveling suit, sports clothes, and accessories for packing. Then she sat down at her desk to write a letter to Ned Nickerson at Emerson University. She and Ned had been friends for several years.

"It would be nice if Ned could come down to Charlottesville while I'm there," Nancy thought, as she picked up her pen.

After telling Ned the news and how she hoped to win the reward for finding the missing stained-glass window, Nancy gave him Susan Carr's address. When she finished the letter, Nancy decided to mail it at once and started for the corner mailbox.

After posting the letter, Nancy walked back. As she reached the house, Togo came bounding

Nancy tried to take the paper from Togo

down the street toward his mistress. In his mouth was a small piece of paper. Nancy leaned over and tried to take it from him.

"So you're not going to give it up?" She laughed as the terrier pranced around.

The game went on for several minutes. Then Togo, apparently deciding to play something else, let Nancy take the paper. It proved to be the upper right-hand section of an envelope. On it was a canceled stamp and the postmark was Charlottesville, Virginia, three days before!

"Togo," said Nancy quickly, "where did you get this?"

The little dog barked excitedly but made no move to show her. A frightening thought occurred to Nancy. Suppose, when Togo had been looking for the missing letters the previous day, he had found the one with the hundred-dollar bill and torn it to pieces!

Worried, she took the dog into the house and told Hannah her fears. "Now I'll really have to solve that mystery," she said. "Maybe the Drew family does owe Mrs. Dondo a hundred dollars!"

"I might believe that if you hadn't overheard what Mr. Dondo said to his wife," Mrs. Gruen replied. "I'm inclined to think that woman is faking the whole thing. Find out what you can about her brother while you're in Charlottesville."

When Mr. Drew returned that evening, he

handed Nancy plane tickets for her and her chums. "You'll fly to Richmond and then go from there by car to Charlottesville."

"I'll wire Susan to meet us, if possible," said Nancy. "She told me to do that."

Nancy sent the telegram, then called Bess and George to tell them about the reservations. "Dad and I will pick you up right after church tomorrow," she said.

The next morning Nancy packed her suitcase early. Her father carried it to the car, then the family ate a leisurely breakfast. They had just finished when the telephone rang. Nancy went to answer the call.

"Miss Nancy Drew?" asked a woman's voice.

"Yes."

"This is Western Union. I have a telegram for you from Charlottesville, Virginia. It's signed *Susan Carr*. The message reads:

" 'Postpone your trip. Will write when convenient for you to visit.' "

CHAPTER V

The Driver's Mask

NANCY sat lost in thought for a few moments. It was not like Susan to send such an ungracious message! After repeating the telegram to her father, Nancy said, "I can't understand it."

Mr. Drew smiled. "Telegrams aren't gracious usually," he said. "It's possible Susan didn't word it." The lawyer laughed. "Maybe her husband did, and men are usually brief in sending messages, you know."

"I suppose I could start somewhere else to hunt for the stained-glass window," Nancy mused. "But I would certainly like to talk to Mr. Bradshaw in Charlottesville."

"Why don't you go anyway?" Mr. Drew suggested. "You can stay at a hotel if it's not convenient for Susan to have you at her home."

"I'll call Bess and George and see if that will be all right with them," Nancy replied.

When Nancy talked to the cousins they both agreed to the new arrangements. Fortunately, each of them had enough money saved to cover the additional expense.

"Fine," Nancy told George, whom she had called last. "Dad and I will be there as scheduled."

After picking up the girls, Mr. Drew drove them to the airport. Soon the great airliner taxied in and the girls climbed aboard. They waved affectionately from the window to Nancy's father, then fastened their seat belts.

The flight was smooth and the plane landed on time at the Richmond airport. After the girls had claimed their luggage, porters carried it to a waiting taxi and they went at once to the Hotel Richmond.

"What a lovely city!" Bess remarked, as they drove through the tree-lined streets and saw one charming colonial house after another, each with a beautiful garden.

When they reached the hotel, Nancy asked for a large room with three beds in it. This type of accommodation was not available, but the desk clerk offered them a single and a double room with connecting bath.

After the bellhops had deposited the girls' bags, George noticed a radio in the large room. "Let's hear the news," she suggested, turning it on.

The local station was broadcasting. As the

girls removed their coats and combed their hair, the announcer gave world-wide events, and next, happenings in the state of Virginia. Then he began relating items of interest in the Richmond area.

Suddenly the girls were electrified by an announcement. "Mrs. Clifford Carr of Charlottesville, while driving to the Richmond airport, was involved in an accident. Her automobile was sideswiped by another car and overturned in a ditch. She was taken to Johnston Willis Hospital. There is no trace of the driver who caused the accident."

"Oh, my goodness!" Nancy cried out. "That's Cousin Susan. We must get to the hospital at once and find out how she is! I hope she's not seriously hurt."

The three girls donned their coats and hurried out to the elevator. Reaching the hotel lobby, they walked quickly to the street and hailed a taxi. As Nancy jumped in, she said to the driver:

"Johnston Willis Hospital!"

The driver, a friendly sort of man, asked, "Is one of you all sick?"

"No, but a friend of ours was in an automobile accident. We'd appreciate getting to the hospital as quickly as possible."

The driver, in a drawl, assured them that he would do his best. His slow pace taxed their patience, but finally they arrived at the hospital.

Nancy led the way inside and at the desk explained to the woman in charge that she was Mrs. Carr's cousin. "I'd like to see her if possible." After several minutes' delay, she was told the number of Susan's room and that she might go upstairs to talk to her cousin.

"Perhaps George and I should wait here," said Bess. "Let us know if Susan can see us."

Nancy hurried upstairs to her cousin's room. Susan, pale, and with bruised forehead and arms, had her eyes closed. Nancy stood at the side of the bed for several seconds before Susan looked up. Then, as if by magic, the young woman's expression changed completely.

"Nancy!" she cried out, and put up her arms to embrace her cousin.

"Hi, Sue!" Nancy said, leaning over to kiss her.

"Oh, I'm so glad you're here," said Susan. "But how did you learn about the accident?"

Nancy told her about the radio broadcast and that Bess and George had come with her to the hospital immediately upon hearing what had happened.

"Where are they?" Susan asked.

"Downstairs."

Susan insisted that they come up at once, so Nancy went to get them. As soon as greetings were exchanged, Susan said she felt better already.

The girls, relieved that her injuries were minor, thought it best not to talk about the accident. Instead, Nancy said:

"You're probably surprised that we came down here after you sent the telegram. But we thought we'd come, anyway, to find out what we could about the missing stained-glass window."

Susan's eyebrows raised. "I didn't send you a telegram," she said. "What do you mean?"

When Nancy explained, a worried frown came over Susan's face. "But why would anyone do such a thing?" she asked. "And who sent it?"

Nancy said she was mystified. Bess and George looked worried. All three girls knew now that someone had deliberately tried to keep Nancy from coming to Charlottesville.

Suddenly another thought occurred to Nancy. Perhaps the same person, knowing the telegram ruse had failed, had also sideswiped Susan's car, hoping to keep Susan from meeting the girls! But what was the reason for keeping them apart?

"Perhaps the culprit hoped to delay me for some time in Richmond. But it was a pretty horrible method to take," she thought angrily.

Hoping to learn more details, Nancy said, "Susan, I had decided not to talk about your accident, but it might have some bearing on the telegram. Do you think that the person who sideswiped you could have done it on purpose?"

"Oh, yes," Susan said immediately. "There

was no one on the road and the man had lots of room to pass. He kept alongside me for several feet. I was so afraid he'd rip off my fender and our wheels would lock, that I kept pulling over.

"The next thing I knew I went into the ditch and turned over. He never stopped to help me. It was quite a few minutes before another car came along. The driver brought me here."

"Did you get a good look at the man who caused the accident?" Nancy asked her cousin.

For answer, Susan closed her eyes and shuddered. "He had a horrible face!" She opened her eyes again, adding, "Nancy, it wasn't a natural face at all—leering and expressionless. You know what I think?"

"That he wore a rubber mask?" Nancy asked.

"Exactly. So there's no chance to identify him."

Bess and George expressed their concern. Susan herself became more alarmed and said, "I have no enemies. Why should a man deliberately cause an accident? I might have been killed!"

"I can't answer that, Sue," Nancy replied, "Have the police been notified?"

"Yes."

"Then," said Nancy, "promise me you'll try to forget the whole thing and get some sleep. How long does the doctor think you'll have to stay here?"

"Oh, I can go home tomorrow. My car was

towed to a garage and will be fixed by that time."

Susan took hold of Nancy's hands and looked at her affectionately. "I'm so glad you came. My husband is away. The doctor notified him that I was all right and he'll be home tomorrow, but in the meantime I felt so alone here. Now I'm much better, thanks to you girls. Don't worry about me. I'll get a good night's sleep and we'll start for Charlottesville tomorrow morning."

The nurse came into the room just then and suggested that the visitors leave, since the patient needed rest. The three said good-by and went back to the hotel.

The rest of the afternoon and evening was spent in viewing the old city with its many historic spots, including the courthouse designed by Thomas Jefferson and old St. John's Church, where Patrick Henry delivered his immortal "Give me liberty or give me death" oration.

As the girls were ready to tumble into bed, Bess remarked with a yawn, "I feel as if I'd had a refresher course in American history!"

After breakfast the next morning Nancy called the hospital and talked with Susan. Her cousin insisted she felt completely recovered. She had just one request, though. She asked Nancy to pick up her convertible at the Blossom Garage, and come to the hospital for her.

"Of course," said Nancy. "See you soon."

The owner of the Blossom Garage was a pleasant man. After Nancy explained why she wanted to take Mrs. Carr's convertible and had shown her driver's license, he said it would be all right.

"How much is the bill?" Nancy asked. The man figured the amount and she paid it.

Nancy seated herself behind the wheel and started off with George and Bess in the back seat. Susan was waiting in front of the hospital and climbed in with Nancy.

About five miles out of town, as they started to round a curve, Nancy suddenly found that the steering apparatus would not work. The wheel spun around wildly! Frantically she jammed on the brakes hard, but could not regain control of the car.

The convertible plunged into an embankment!

CHAPTER VI

A Desperate Enemy

THROWN forward by the impact, the car's passengers were stunned. Nancy had been able to brace herself against the steering wheel. Bess and George in the rear seat had fallen to the floor, but were not injured.

Susan, however, had been flung hard against the windshield. To Nancy's horror, she saw her cousin slump down and black out!

"Oh, Sue!" she cried, leaning over and easing her cousin lengthwise on the seat. Nancy was fearful that another shock, coming so closely on the heels of the one the day before, might have a severe effect on Susan.

By this time Bess and George had picked themselves up. They, too, were aghast to see Susan unconscious.

"Are you girls all right?" Nancy asked them.

"Yes."

"We must get Sue to a doctor right away," said Nancy. "I think we passed a doctor's home about a quarter of a mile back. I'll walk there and ask him to come here with me."

"I'll go," George offered, "while you and Bess see what you can do for Susan." She opened the car door and started off at once.

"I see a brook over there," Bess spoke up. "I'll get some water."

She hurried to the brook and wet her handkerchief. Returning, she laid it on Susan's forehead. Presently the young woman's eyelids flickered open. She looked around dazedly, then asked, "Where am I?"

"We had a little accident," Nancy replied soothingly. "George has gone for a doctor. Sue, just lie still."

Wearily Susan closed her eyes again. By the time she felt able to open them, they heard a car coming down the road. A moment later it stopped behind Susan's automobile and George alighted. She was followed by a tall man who carried a physician's bag.

Nodding to the others, he came at once to Susan's side and began to examine her. Taking a tablet from his bag, he put it in her mouth and told her to let it dissolve on her tongue.

"You're all very fortunate," he said, looking at the car, rammed into the embankment. "This young lady will be all right. She's had a bad shock, but nothing's broken and there is no sign of a concussion. I suggest that you all come back with me to my house and take it easy while we see what can be done for your car."

The girls accepted with alacrity, adding they would like to take their luggage along. The physician, whom George now introduced as Dr. Steyer, readily agreed and helped transfer the bags to his automobile.

"As soon as we reach home, I'll put in a call to a service garage," he offered.

When a mechanic arrived a few minutes later, Nancy drove with him to Susan's car. She told him that she suspected the steering mechanism had not been properly repaired after the accident the day before.

"I'll soon find out," the young man said.

When they reached Susan's convertible, he went to work at once. Presently he said that either the steering assembly had not been tested or had been tampered with later.

"In any case, the car's in bad shape and you won't be able to drive it until the grill and front wheels are straightened and a whole new steering assembly is put in."

Nancy asked the mechanic if he would arrange to have Susan's automobile towed to his garage. "Mrs. Carr will let you know what she wants done with it," Nancy added.

He agreed and drove her back to Dr. Steyer's house.

When Nancy told the others of the mechanic's report, Susan became very upset. Up to now, she had remained reasonably calm, but suddenly she began to cry hysterically.

"That masked man did it!" she cried out. "I don't know why, but he's trying to kill me!"

Nancy put her arm around her cousin's shoulders and tried to comfort her. But the young woman seemed to be totally unnerved.

"That face! That awful face!" Susan suddenly laughed. Then the next moment she was weeping. "We might have injured a lot of people!"

"Please, Sue," Nancy begged her cousin, "try to calm yourself."

Finally, Dr. Steyer gave Susan a sedative with some water. A few minutes later she lay back on a couch and went to sleep.

"She'll wake up in about an hour feeling completely refreshed and a lot steadier," the physician said.

His wife, who had been shopping, now came in. He introduced her, and when Mrs. Steyer heard the story, kindly offered to drive all the girls to Charlottesville.

"I was planning to go over there this afternoon," she said, "and I'll be very happy to have company."

Nancy thanked her, then Mrs. Steyer invited

them all to have lunch with her and the doctor. Bess and George offered to help.

"That's very kind of you girls," Mrs. Steyer said, "but it would break my Mandy's heart. She's my faithful maid who has been with the family for nearly fifty years."

Mandy proved to be a delightful colored woman. When she heard what had happened, she became very motherly.

"That's a shame. And you all ain't got no kinfolk down here to help you out o' this trouble," she cooed. "But Mandy'll see to it you all have a good lunch. Then I knows everyone o' you will feel better."

While the meal was being prepared, Nancy telephoned the Blossom Garage in Richmond and spoke to the owner. After hearing her story of the morning's accident, the man said, "Hold the line a minute. I'll check our records."

A few minutes later he reported that not only had the steering assembly of Susan's car been checked, but that there was a notation on the report that it had been in perfect condition.

"Then what do you think happened?" Nancy queried.

The garage owner said it was possible that the accident might be accounted for by a strange incident which had happened late the previous night.

"My watchman reported that he heard muffled

hammering in a far corner of the building. When he went to investigate, he saw a man sneak out of the building. It's just possible the fellow damaged your car, but of course this is only a guess."

Nancy hung up. She felt sure that the man's surmise had been correct. This heightened the mystery. If Susan had no enemies, it seemed obvious that the strange man was trying to injure Nancy, Bess, and George.

"The only reason for that would be to keep us from Charlottesville," she said to herself. "But why?"

The thought of Alonzo Rugby being responsible flitted through her mind, but Nancy dismissed it at once. The loss of a hundred dollars was not provocation for such drastic retaliation!

"But who is the person?" she kept asking herself. "Whoever he is, the man must be pretty desperate."

Susan awoke just as lunch was to be served. She declared that she felt completely recovered and apologized for the way she had acted.

"I guess two accidents were two too many," she said, smiling wryly.

Susan, as well as the others, ate heartily and praised Mandy for her excellent cooking. Directly after lunch, Mrs. Steyer brought her car from the garage and the group set off for Charlottesville.

The girls found the countryside, with its attractive farm lands and grazing horses, most delightful. As they entered Charlottesville, Mrs. Steyer asked:

"Where do you live, Mrs. Carr?"

Susan gave directions. Her home, Seven Oaks, was about three miles out of town, and had been in her husband's family for many years.

"I felt very fortunate moving into such a beautiful house as a bride," she remarked, smiling.

When they reached it, Nancy and her chums gazed in delight. A low brick wall ran across the front of the small estate. An iron gateway opened onto a tree-shaded drive with beautiful, many-hued flower gardens on either side of it.

Facing the end of the drive was a white clapboard two-story colonial house. At the entrance was a small porch with Doric columns. Above the entrance was a balcony which Susan said opened off her bedroom.

"It's perfectly charming!" Nancy exclaimed enthusiastically.

As the girls thanked Mrs. Steyer and alighted from the car, the front door of the house was opened by a plump, smiling colored woman.

"Land sakes, Miss Susan!" she cried. "You done scared me half to death! It's mighty good to see you walking around."

"And I'm glad to *be* walking around," Susan Carr replied. "Beulah, this is Miss Nancy Drew,

Miss Bess Marvin, and Miss George Fayne."

Beulah was too polite to ask how George happened to have a boy's name, but she gave the girl a second glance which clearly indicated her puzzlement.

"Now don't you worry none about the luggage," said Beulah as the girls lifted their bags from Mrs. Steyer's car. "I'll have them up to your rooms in a jiffy."

She picked up all three suitcases at once and went into the house with them.

Nancy and her friends followed Susan.

There was a large center hall with the paneling and all woodwork painted white, except for the mahogany railing of the curved stairway. A flowered wallpaper and thick carpeting made the entrance most welcoming.

To the right was the living room, and to the left a library which Cliff Carr used as his office. There was a sunny dining room back of the living room and an open porch beyond this.

"And now I'll show you to your rooms," said Susan, and led the way upstairs.

The three adjoining bedrooms, papered in dainty colonial patterns and each with a fireplace, were charming. Nancy's room had an antique four-poster bed, with a red and white patchwork quilt covering it.

Susan said she would meet the girls downstairs. After they had unpacked and changed their clothes, the three of them gazed out at the beautifully landscaped grounds at the rear of the property.

Beds of various kinds of flowers, surrounded by low boxwood hedges, were interlaced with brick paths which ran throughout the garden.

"Cliff is certainly a good ad for his profession of landscape architecture," said George.

Nancy nodded. "He completely renovated this whole estate just before he and Sue were married."

Bess took a deep breath. "It smells simply heavenly!" she said. "I'm afraid I'll never want to go home."

By the time they went downstairs, Susan's sandy-haired, six-foot husband had come in. Nancy had not seen Cliff since the wedding, and Bess and George had never met him.

After some general conversation, he turned to Nancy. "You've come at exactly the right time," he said. "There's a neighborhood mystery to be solved."

There was an involuntary groan from George. "Not another?" she said under her breath.

Cliff laughed. "Susan told me about the stained-glass window and the fake telegram," he said. "But surely you can add one more to the list." Apparently he had purposely left out any reference to the car accidents.

"Tell me what the mystery is," Nancy begged.

"We have a neighbor named Mr. Honsho, from India. A couple of years ago he bought one of the most beautiful old estates around here."

"It's called Cumberland Manor," Susan said. "Mr. Honsho spoiled it by putting a high wall around the grounds, and no one has been allowed inside since!"

Cliff took up the story. "Nancy, mysterious sounds come from the place day and night. And well—the fact is—we want you to solve the mystery."

"And for a very special reason," Susan added.

Nancy waited intently to hear what it was.

CHAPTER VII

The Telltale Magazine

ALL eyes turned on Susan as the girls waited for her announcement. During the pause which followed, Bess said, "Oh, I hope it isn't something gruesome."

"The mystery may be," Susan warned her. "Before Mr. Honsho bought the place, it was always open to the public for Garden Week. Nancy, we'd like you to find out what those horrible screeches are, stop them, and persuade the owner to permit visitors."

"A big assignment," George remarked.

"Yes, it is," said Cliff. "Some of the men around Charlottesville have tried and the Garden Tour group, too. But so far we've failed."

"Well, count me out," Bess spoke up. "I'll help with something that's not so weird."

"Then suppose you take over the case of Mrs. Dondo's brother," said Nancy, her eyes twinkling mischievously.

"No, thank you," Bess answered quickly. "If any men are coming into my life, I want them to be young and handsome. I don't think any brother of hers could meet either of those requirements." The others laughed.

When Nancy said she wanted to go to Mr. Bradshaw's studio as soon as possible, Cliff generously offered to lend the girls his car the following day.

"I'll be working in my office here and shan't need it. Why don't you go to Bradshaw's after you see Mr. Honsho? When you leave Cumberland Manor, keep driving on the same road and you'll come to the studio. The two places are not far apart. In fact, they're both on Eddy Run."

When Bess looked puzzled at this last remark, Cliff explained that Eddy Run was a swift-moving creek that flowed past the rear of the properties.

"You'll be able to find Mr. Honsho's place easily," he said. "Take the road to Charlottesville and at the first intersection turn right. That road will lead directly to Cumberland Manor."

The following morning after breakfast, the three girls started off in Cliff's station wagon. On reaching Mr. Honsho's estate, they gazed at the high brick wall which Susan had mentioned. The entrance gate was of solid iron, completely screening even a glimpse of the interior. Nancy noticed a bell at the side of the gate, stopped the car, and got out to ring it. There was no answer to her summons.

"I'd say Mr. Honsho just doesn't want visitors," Bess remarked. "Well, Nancy, you can't solve this mystery now, so let's go on."

But Nancy was reluctant to give up so easily. She drove to the point where the brick wall turned toward Eddy Run, and stopped. "Let's walk down alongside the wall," she urged. "We may come to another entrance."

She and the cousins walked along a dirt path which skirted the brick enclosure. Bicycle tire tracks were evident and a few minutes later the girls saw a young man on a bicycle stopping at a high wooden door. Dismounting, he took a key from his pocket.

Nancy started to run and in a few seconds came close enough to attract his attention. He looked up at her in surprise. About twenty-five years of age, he was tall and slender, with reddish hair and blue eyes. He wore a work shirt, jeans, and a cowboy belt.

On seeing Nancy, the young man looked frightened. He quickly inserted the key in the lock, opened the door, and shoved his bicycle inside.

"Please wait!" Nancy cried out. "I want to talk with you!"

The young man paid no attention to her request. He let himself in quickly, slammed the door, and the girls heard the lock click. By this time Bess and George had reached their friend.

"I wonder who he is," said George.

"He must work at Cumberland Manor," Nancy remarked. "Probably he has instructions from his employer not to talk to strangers and certainly not to let them into the grounds."

Bess giggled. "You haven't had a man slam a door in your face for a long time, Nancy," she teased.

"No, not since her last mystery," George added.

The words were hardly out of her mouth when from inside the estate came a horrible screech. Then there was an ominous silence.

Bess cowered against the other girls. "Somebody's being tortured in there!"

"If so," said Nancy, "we must try to help the person!"

"But how," said Bess, "when we can't even get inside the place?"

Nancy admitted that she was stymied. The screech, which had sounded somewhat like a screaming tomcat, although much more foreboding, was not repeated.

"I think I know what it may have been," Nancy said. "A peacock!"

"What makes you think so?" George asked.

Nancy explained that she had read a lot about peacocks after she had decided to look for the old stained-glass window. "From the description of the bird's screech, it would sound like what we just heard."

Bess was not convinced and declared that Mr. Honsho's activities should be reported to the police. "I'm going back to the car," she declared.

Nancy and George wanted to do some more sleuthing. They continued along the path which led all the way to Eddy Run. To their disappointment, the brick wall was as high across the water side of Cumberland Manor as the section they had just seen. And it contained no opening. Feeling sure that the far side of the estate would have no unlocked gate, they gave up and started back to the car.

As the girls approached it, Bess heaved a sigh. "I was getting worried about you two," she said. "Any luck?"

"No. Mr. Honsho sure keeps himself hidden away from the outside world."

Nancy admitted that it was going to be most difficult to try contacting the Indian. "And Garden Week isn't far off," she said, frowning. "But we'll go on to Mr. Bradshaw's now." She and George climbed into the car and they headed for Waverly.

On the way to the studio, they passed another estate. Apparently it had once been an attractive place, but now it showed signs of neglect.

Though the beech trees along the roadway were large and beautiful, the property was edged with a tumble-down stone wall and closely matted vines.

"There's the name," said Bess. "Ivy Hall."

About half a mile beyond was the entrance to Waverly. The grounds reminded the girls of farms outside River Heights. There was no wall and few trees. A roadway wound among well-kept lawns and fields.

Nearing a rambling farmhouse, Nancy spotted a sign with an arrow which indicated that Mr. Mark Bradshaw's studio was at the rear of the property.

Nancy continued down a lane. To the left of it were lovely flower gardens and to the right a dense woods. A short distance from Eddy Run, and standing under the branches of a giant spreading oak, was the studio. It was a long, brick building almost completely covered with English ivy.

The studio door stood open. As Nancy parked, a man in his late forties, wearing a smock and horn-rimmed glasses, came outside. He was thin and intense-looking, and his dark hair was cut boyishly short. In a low, vibrant voice he said:

"How do you do?"

"Mr. Bradshaw?" Nancy asked.

When the man nodded, she introduced herself and her friends. She told him they were interested in stained-glass windows, and had learned a little about the art from Mr. Atwater who had a studio near them in River Heights.

Mr. Bradshaw invited them into the studio, which looked very much like Mr. Atwater's. "Is there something in particular you wish to learn?" he asked, smiling pleasantly.

Quickly Nancy explained about the article in the *Continental* and asked if he had heard about it. When he said no, she gave him the details of the story.

"I'd like to solve the mystery and donate the reward money to our hospital," she said.

"That is a very laudable ambition," the artist said. "But how can I help you?"

Nancy mentioned her cousin Susan Carr and at once Mr. Bradshaw's face lighted up. "A delightful young woman!" he said. "My wife and I enjoy Mr. and Mrs. Carr very much. Cliff is a clever fellow. I'll be more than happy to help their cousin locate this missing window. Let's see how we can go about it."

"First, perhaps, you could tell us where some of the famous works of stained-glass art are located in this area." Nancy said.

Mr. Bradshaw shook his head. "I'm very sorry, but I'm not too well versed on that. But I would be glad to tell you about the art itself. The more you know of the process, the better able you'll be to recognize the genuine article if you find it."

Walking to a spot near a large window, Mr. Bradshaw uncovered an easel on which stood a very attractive stained-glass picture of a modern hunting scene. The artist explained that it was to be put in the home of a friend in Washington.

"Actually," he said, "a stained-glass window is a translucent mosaic held together by lead. But the lead between the sections is not just a fancy glue. It plays a real part in the design."

"The leading is almost the last thing which is done, isn't it?" Nancy asked Mr. Bradshaw.

"Almost," the man replied. "The final step is the cementing which holds the leading and the glass together."

"Would you mind explaining the cutting table, Mr. Bradshaw?" George requested. "All I know about it is that one should be careful of glass pieces lying on top." She gazed ruefully at the scar on the palm of her right hand.

"Why, certainly," said the artist graciously.

He led the way to one of two benches which stood at the far end of the room. Each was solidly built and had a thick plate-glass top. "This," he explained, "ensures a constantly flat surface which is of utmost importance in the cutting process."

Beneath it a large mirror was tilted diagonally

from the front edge of the table to the back of a shelf below. A light on the mirror gave a brilliance which was helpful to the cutter when he worked with dark glass.

"And this," said Mr. Bradshaw, picking up an odd-looking tool, "is a wheel glass cutter. The square-grooved sections have the funny name of nibbling mouths."

As he was speaking, Nancy caught sight of a magazine carelessly thrown behind one of the benches. The advertisement on the back was the same as that on the copy of the *Continental* which she had seen in River Heights.

Unnoticed by the others, she slid her foot under the bench and flipped the magazine over. It was the same issue of the *Continental* as the one which carried the story of the missing stained-glass window!

Nancy was amazed. Surely Mr. Bradshaw must have seen the article. Then why had he denied knowing about it?

A sudden thought struck the young detective. Bradshaw might already be searching for the window himself!

CHAPTER VIII

The Paint Clue

NANCY wondered if Mr. Bradshaw might know where the peacock window was.

Suddenly Bess realized that Nancy was not paying strict attention to the artist. Wondering why, she followed the other girl's gaze and saw the magazine. Instantly she knew Nancy was suspicious. Bess also noticed that Mr. Bradshaw was looking in the young detective's direction.

To warn her friend, Bess said, "Isn't this talk fascinating, Nancy? I had no idea that the art of making stained-glass windows was so intricate."

With a grateful smile at Bess, Nancy nodded and replied, "Yes, it's extremely interesting. But to me, designing the picture would be the most intriguing part."

Mr. Bradshaw's eyes lighted up. "I agree with you a hundred per cent, Miss Drew. And it is probably the most difficult part. Beginners can rarely fashion a picture which is feasible to be used for a stained-glass window. It takes a great deal of practice to plan a design which will cut into the right-shaped pieces."

Presently, not wanting to take any more of Mr. Bradshaw's time, they told him how much they appreciated his courtesy and help, then said good-by.

He smiled at them warmly and said, "The pleasure has been mine."

As the girls drove off, Bess at once mentioned the *Continental* and asked Nancy if she thought Mr. Bradshaw knew more than he was willing to admit.

"Yes, I do."

George, after hearing about the magazine, remarked, "Well, I can't blame him for wanting to win the reward himself." Then she asked, "Nancy did you learn anything that might help *you* find the window?"

"Nothing in particular," her friend answered. "But I have a hunch it's in this area."

"Do you think Mr. Bradshaw knows where it is?" Bess questioned.

"Probably not."

"Then it may still be a race," said George enthusiastically. "And I hope you win!"

At the Carr home the girls found Susan in the living room studying picture pamphlets of various automobiles. She looked up at them and smiled.

"What do you think?" she said excitedly. "Cliff wants me to get a new car."

"You're lucky," said Bess. "Have you decided what kind of car to get?"

Susan had not made up her mind and was waiting for the girls' advice. "What kind do you all have?" she asked.

Each of the three girls' families had a different make, but both Bess and George declared that Nancy's convertible was their favorite. "If you get one like hers, you'll love it," Bess added.

Susan stood up and said impulsively, "I'll do it. Come on down to the showroom with me and we'll see what they have."

Within an hour they were back at Seven Oaks, with Susan driving her new convertible. George, who had ridden back with her, stepped from the new beige-and-blue automobile.

"Hypers, this is a record for buying a new car!" she said, laughing.

Nancy and Bess arrived in the station wagon just as Cliff came out to inspect the new purchase. He congratulated his wife on her fine selection, then said to Nancy: "For the duration of your stay here you're welcome to use either of our cars. There's only one condition attached."

"What's that?"

"You must solve at least one mystery while you're here."

Nancy laughed merrily, then asked Susan and

Cliff how plans were coming for Garden Week.

"Everything is about ready," Cliff answered. "But the committee is disappointed that the owner of Cumberland Manor still refuses to open it to the public."

"I'm sorry I didn't have better luck on the first try," said Nancy. "But perhaps I can think of another method of approach."

As the girls entered the front hall of the house, Nancy noticed that a letter addressed to her was lying on a mahogany table. It was from Hannah Gruen.

As Nancy read it she frowned. Mrs. Dondo was trying to make trouble again! The woman had been telling people in River Heights that Nancy had left town to avoid paying the hundred dollars which had been lost in the mail. Then suddenly Nancy smiled as she read further. Hannah had written:

"But don't worry, Nancy. Your father is taking care of things. He went over to her house and talked to her sternly. Mrs. Dondo actually began to tremble and said she would not say anything more against you."

Nancy reread the letter, then went upstairs. When Bess and George came into her room, Nancy told them the contents of the letter.

"Well good for your dad!" said Bess. "That woman needs to be put in her place."

George looked up. "But I'm afraid she won't

keep her promise. Nancy, you'd better watch out!"

The girls continued to discuss the unpleasant woman and her brother. When they joined Susan and Cliff on the patio just before dusk, Nancy asked them if they had ever heard of Alonzo Rugby.

Both of them shook their heads and Cliff looked in the telephone directory. The name was not listed.

"He's an artist," Nancy explained.

"In that case," said Cliff, "the head of the University art department might help us. I'll call him."

He went inside to phone. When Cliff returned, he reported that Alonzo Rugby was not known to the department head.

"That's strange," Nancy remarked. "We were told that he's a talented artist." Then she related to the Carrs the story Mrs. Dondo had told about her brother who was supposed to live in Charlottesville.

Obligingly Cliff telephoned an art dealer in town, then Susan called a woman artist in the area. Neither of them had ever heard of Alonzo Rugby.

"Oh, let's forget him," Bess suggested, "and enjoy this heavenly evening."

Nancy did not reply; she knew she could not forget the man. The young detective had a strong hunch that he had been responsible for the fake telegram to her. His only reason for sending it must have been to keep her out of the area. But why?

"If he's 'good for nothing,' as his brother-in-law says," Nancy thought, "he may be involved in some underhanded scheme. But where do I fit in?"

Just then melodic chimes sounded from inside the house. Beulah always rang these to announce dinner. The group arose and went inside.

The colonial dining room of Seven Oaks was charming. A crystal chandelier highlighted the handsome mahogany furniture, as well as the exquisite silver candelabra and crystal tumblers on the table.

Clifford said grace, then Beulah brought in a heavy silver tureen of soup which she set before Susan. Next, she brought in lovely old china soup plates. One by one she passed them after Susan had served the portions.

When the maid left the room, Susan smiled and whispered to the girls, "I try to make things easier for Beulah but she insists upon working and serving everything the old-fashioned way. I must confess, though, that I love it."

Cliff's eyes twinkled. "Beulah's a rare person," he said. "She sort of lives in the past, and is very much like her mother, who worked for my mother. She imitates her in everything."

Beulah shrieked and pointed to the window

After the soup course, Beulah brought in a tray of squabs and remarked to the visitors, "I hope you all like my birds."

The "birds" proved to be delicious, as well as the sweet potatoes, corn pudding, and piping hot biscuits served with them.

Bess said happily, "Don't anybody remind me I'm on a diet!"

Twenty minutes later Beulah removed the dishes and carried in individual servings of strawberry shortcake. She had brought in all but Cliff's piece, and was just returning from the pantry with it, when suddenly she shrieked. The dessert slipped from her hand and turned upside down on the floor.

"Lawsy me!" she cried out, wringing her hands.

Those at the table stared at the woman in amazement. Beulah pointed toward an open side window. "A man with eyes of the devil was lookin' in here. He was tryin' to cast a spell on all of us!"

Everyone jumped up and hurried out to the garden in back of the house. It was too dark to see much, but they could hear running footsteps in the distance.

"I suppose it would be hopeless to try to catch the fellow," Cliff remarked.

Nancy said nothing. She was thinking. Perhaps she could pick up some clue to the man's identity. Returning to the house, she hurried to her room and took a flashlight from her suitcase.

By this time the others had come indoors. Susan was trying to assure Beulah, who was on the verge of hysterics, that probably the man had meant no harm.

Nancy, meanwhile, had easily spotted the man's footprints under the window. They led alongside one of the garden paths. About a hundred feet from the house she spotted a small metal tube and picked it up. She read:

BLACK

(oxide of iron)

"An artist dropped this!" she thought excitedly. Instantly her mind flew to Mark Bradshaw, then to Alonzo Rugby. "I must tell Bess and George!"

Nancy turned to go back. At the same moment something hard hit her squarely between the shoulders. She fell forward and lost consciousness!

CHAPTER IX

Jigsaw in Glass

INSIDE the house Bess, George, and the Carrs were talking excitedly about the man who had peered in the window. When Beulah gave a description of his face, Susan was sure he was the masked man who had caused her first automobile accident.

"I'll call the police," Cliff said, and went to the phone.

Dessert had been forgotten, but suddenly the cook remembered that "her folks" had not eaten the strawberry shortcake.

"I'll fix another helpin' for Mr. Cliff right away," she said. "You all go back to the dinin' room, so I can hustle."

It was not until they returned to their places at the table that the group realized Nancy had not joined them.

"That's odd," said George. "I saw her come into the house."

She went to the foot of the stairs and called to the second floor. There was no answer. Worried, George went up and looked around. Coming down, she remarked to the others:

"Nancy must have gone outdoors again to do some sleuthing."

"Oh, dear," said Susan, "I hope nothing has happened to her!"

Cliff hurried for a flashlight and the group went outside. Casting the light around, Cliff soon spotted the man's footprints. Figuring that Nancy had trailed him, the group followed the marks and soon came upon the girl's limp form.

"Oh, Nancy!" Bess cried out, terrified. She fell to her knees beside the stricken girl.

To Bess's intense relief, Nancy at this moment opened her eyes. She blinked in the glare of the flashlight and mumbled, "Where is the— the—paint tube?"

The onlookers glanced at one another worriedly. Was Nancy delirious? But a moment later her mind cleared and she sat up.

"Something hit me in the back. I fell forward, hit my head, and blacked out," she said, looking around. Pointing to a large stone, she added, "I guess someone threw that at me."

"How awful!" Susan exclaimed. Then she

told Nancy her suspicion that the man was the one who had shoved her car off the road.

"And he was an artist, I think," said Nancy. She told them of the tube of black paint. "He apparently knocked me out to get it away from me without being seen. Anyway, it's gone."

The Carrs, puzzled and worried, helped Nancy to her feet and they all went into the house. Nancy was immediately put to bed. Not only the police but the Carrs' physician, whom Susan summoned, arrived in a few minutes.

Dr. Tillett, solicitous and efficient, examined Nancy and announced that she had no serious injuries. He predicted that her back would feel sore for several days, but it would not be necessary for her to stay in bed.

"Just take it easy tomorrow," he advised.

Nancy did not see the police—Cliff had felt it was not necessary and the officers had agreed. But later, when she was alone with Bess and George, the young sleuth remarked:

"The tube of paint was a good clue."

"You suspect that Bradshaw or Rugby dropped it?" asked George.

"Yes, I do."

Nancy said that the next morning she was going to make a paper model of one or two of the footprints. "Then I'll pay another visit to Waverly as soon as I can and see if by any chance Bradshaw's shoe might fit the print."

"Good idea," said George, "but it won't be easy to do."

"I know," said Nancy, yawning wearily, "but I'm going to try it."

The following morning Bess and George helped her make the paper footprint. Luckily the ground was hard enough to permit this. Because of the Carrs' friendship with Bradshaw, the girls did not tell Susan or Cliff what they had in mind.

At luncheon Susan said, "I have an idea. This afternoon we might visit some of the old estates around here. How would you like to see Thomas Jefferson's and James Monroe's homes?"

"Oh, we'd love it!" Bess replied for all the girls.

"And if we have time," Susan went on, "we'll visit some other interesting old places. As we go along, Nancy, you might inquire of people about the missing stained-glass window."

Nancy was thrilled to make the trip and the sightseers set off at once. As they drove along, Susan reminded the others that Thomas Jefferson, the third president of the United States, had served as American minister to France. While there he had become interested in Roman architecture by observing famous ruins. After his return to Virginia, he had designed his home, Monticello, in this style.

"And he was an inventor, too," Susan remarked.

After leaving the car in the visitors' parking lot, the girls walked up to the stately mansion which stood on a knoll overlooking the rolling Virginia hills. Finally, turning reluctantly away from the lovely view, they went inside the house. There they admired the beautifully proportioned rooms and the many inventions and conveniences which Jefferson had installed in his home.

One arrangement, in particular, attracted the girls. This was a bed, set in a space between two rooms, so that Mr. Jefferson could get out on either side, depending on whether he wanted to be in his dressing room or in his study. During the day the bed could be drawn into the ceiling to allow free circulation of air between the two rooms.

"That's for me!" exclaimed Bess. "You'd never get out on the wrong side of the bed in the morning!"

"Let's go on now to James Monroe's home," Susan suggested. "You'll find it more simple, but the gardens have the most beautiful boxwood you've ever seen."

Back in the car again, they drove up the winding mountain road until they came to Ash Lawn. James Monroe, the fifth president of the United States, had built it here to be near his friend Thomas Jefferson.

As Susan had told them, Ash Lawn was smaller

and more informal. A path lined with beautiful boxwood hedges led up to the door. Inside, a mirror hanging on the opposite wall reflected the path, making it appear extremely long.

After leaving Ash Lawn, Susan took the girls to three other estates. At each one Nancy inquired of the owner whether he had heard of any medieval stained-glass windows in the area which had a peacock in the design. In each case the answer was no.

"I guess we'll have to give up for today," said Susan, glancing at the car clock. "It's getting late."

The girls agreed and they started home. Susan had driven only two miles when suddenly she exclaimed, "Why didn't I think of this before!"

"Think of what?" Nancy asked.

"The Dowds. They live right around the next bend. They have a perfectly fascinating home and Mrs. Dowd knows just about everything in the neighborhood. If that window is in any home around the Charlottesville area, she'll know it!"

"Then let's talk to her!" Nancy urged.

Susan turned into the winding driveway of the Dowd place and presently pulled up in front of a rather austere, white-painted-brick mansion. Fortunately Mrs. Dowd, a woman of fifty, was at home. She greeted Susan effusively.

"And bless you, dear, you've brought some *very* attractive friends," she said. Susan introduced them.

Mrs. Dowd proved to be a great talker and the girls did not have a chance to say anything. She expressed her delight at meeting the visitors from River Heights and instantly mentioned two or three people she knew there. Mrs. Dowd bubbled along in the one-sided conversation until finally Susan interrupted diplomatically.

"Nancy would like to ask you some questions," she said.

"Yes, dear, go ahead," said Mrs. Dowd. "What is it you want to know, dear?"

Nancy quickly told her, and to the girl's elation Mrs. Dowd said, "Well, I declare! Now maybe I can lead you all right to that reward."

Her eyes glistened excitedly. "You know, up in our attic, piled in one corner, are the makin's of a stained-glass window. It was hangin' up once. I admit to bein' a right lazy individual when it comes to workin' out puzzles, so I've never tried puttin' the old thing together."

She arose and invited her guests to follow her to the attic. All the way up to the third floor she kept apologizing about the dust and cobwebs which they probably would find, because it was so difficult to get servants these days.

"And as for myself," said Mrs. Dowd, "I never go near the place!"

Fortunately, there were bright lights in the attic and a large cleared space in the center. At once the girls brought the glass sections to this spot and got down on their hands and knees to try figuring out how the various pieces would fit to make a picture. Mrs. Dowd became so excited that she got down and helped them.

"This is a jigsaw puzzle on a large scale," George remarked.

"And just about as hard," Bess added.

By the end of an hour a large section of the window had been put together. Though the picture was not complete, it was evident to the girls that the stained-glass window did not portray a knight riding a white horse and carrying a shield on which there was a peacock.

Finally Nancy stood up. "Mrs. Dowd," she said, "you've been a wonderful sport letting us raid your attic and work on this. But this is not the window we're looking for. Would you like us to put the pieces back where they were?"

"Oh, no, indeed," said Mrs. Dowd. "I declare I'm going to finish this if it takes me a year! I've always been curious to know what this little old window was. I'll get my husband to help me finish puttin' the pieces together."

The girls then followed Mrs. Dowd down the stairs. As they said good-by to her, she wished them luck in finding the right window.

The road to Susan's home led directly past the

Bradshaw farm. Nancy, who had put the paper model of the footprint in her purse, said, "Susan, if it's not too near dinnertime, let's call on Mr. Bradshaw. I'd like to ask him a couple of questions."

"All right." Susan turned in at Waverly, saying, "You know I've been in the Bradshaw home several times, but I've never visited the studio. It will be interesting to see it."

As before, the door stood open and Bradshaw came to greet his visitors. "Susan!" he cried out in delight. "I'm so glad to see you and your friends also."

The callers stepped out of the car and walked into the studio. A man of about forty was standing by the bench under which she had found the copy of *Continental*. He was short, dark, and had very bright small eyes. Mr. Bradshaw waved toward the stranger and said to his callers:

"I'd like to present my new assistant. He has been with me a week. This is Mr. Alonzo Rugby."

CHAPTER X

An Angry Suspect

BESS was so startled to hear the name of the man for whom the girls were searching that she gave a little gasp and stepped back. Alonzo Rugby's eyes narrowed suspiciously as he came forward to acknowledge the introduction. Mr. Bradshaw looked to Susan and the girls for an explanation before giving their names to his assistant.

"I—I'm dreadfully sorry," said Bess, recovering herself. She gave a nervous giggle. "I've heard Mr. Rugby is a famous artist. I was impressed to think I was actually meeting him."

Mr. Bradshaw raised his eyebrows but did not comment. He introduced the girls to Rugby.

"I'm happy to meet you," the assistant said. "I don't know where you heard about my being a great artist. The person must have me mixed up with Mr. Bradshaw. *He's* a great artist. I'm merely a pupil."

Nancy was pleased that at last she had found Mrs. Dondo's brother. "The first thing I must do is try to find out if his shoes fit my paper pattern," she thought.

Nancy noticed that Rugby had taken off his street shoes and put on soft slippers. If she could only find some way to compare the size and shape, as well as those of Mr. Bradshaw's, with her paper pattern!

The young sleuth decided that the best way to accomplish this and to watch both men would be to visit the studio as often as possible. As an idea came to her, she said aloud:

"Mr. Bradshaw, I'm terribly intrigued by stained-glass windowmaking. I was wondering if you would mind giving me a few lessons while I'm visiting my cousin?"

The artist looked surprised, and did not reply at once. Alonzo Rugby, however, said bluntly, "Mr. Bradshaw is not only a great artist but a very busy man, Miss Drew."

Nancy was fearful that Mr. Bradshaw, backed by his assistant, might refuse her request.

But Susan Carr came to her rescue. Smiling at Mr. Bradshaw, she said coaxingly, "Oh, Nancy is not a beginner. She has attended art school."

If Mr. Bradshaw had been wavering in his decision, he was persuaded by this remark. "All right," he said. "I'll be happy to give you a few lessons. Suppose you come tomorrow morning."

Nancy was thrilled. Not only could she learn something from this very fine artist, but perhaps she could unravel the mystery about Mrs. Dondo's brother.

"If he's as bad as Mr. Dondo says, I'm surprised that Mr. Bradshaw would be associating with him," Nancy said to herself. Then a troubling thought struck her. Were the two men in league?

"It doesn't seem possible," she decided. "Mr. Bradshaw is such a gentleman." Aloud she said, "I'll be here by ten o'clock. Thank you so much, Mr. Bradshaw."

The girl detective had come close to the artist. Now she surreptitiously put her own foot near his and glanced down to make some quick mental measurements. It looked as if Mr. Bradshaw could definitely be eliminated as the suspect who had injured her.

Nancy maneuvered to get near Alonzo Rugby's street shoes which he had placed under the bench. She accomplished this when he walked away. As Nancy slid one foot alongside the pair, her heart leaped. The man would bear further investigation!

While Mr. Bradshaw was showing the group a cartoon on which he was working, Alonzo Rugby took Bess by the arm and led her aside. Out of hearing of the others, he whispered:

"I want to give you a warning, miss. Don't let

your friend come here to take lessons. Mr. Bradshaw's wife is the jealous type. A couple of times when he's had women students she made life miserable for them. So you had better keep your friend away from here!"

Bess asked airily, "How do I know this is true?"

Alonzo Rugby said she would have to take his word for it. Before he could add anything, Mr. Bradshaw turned around.

"Better get back to the cutting table, Alonzo," he said pleasantly. "We need that glass for tomorrow morning."

Alonzo immediately returned to his work and Bess joined the others. A few minutes later Susan and her friends left the studio. As they rode toward Seven Oaks, Nancy asked Bess what she and Alonzo had been talking about.

"Making a date?" George asked flippantly.

Bess blushed and said indignantly, "Of course not! But, Nancy, you mustn't go there and take lessons from Mr. Bradshaw!"

"Why not?" Nancy asked in amazement, and Bess repeated Rugby's warning.

At once Susan said, "Why, that's utterly ridiculous. Alicia Bradshaw is one of the loveliest women I know. She most certainly is not the jealous type and never interferes with his work."

Bess looked uncomfortable and her cousin chided her. "I'm surprised at your falling for such a story," George said.

"Well, I'm glad it happened," said Nancy. "Bess has been a bigger help than you give her credit for, George. This convinces me that Alonzo Rugby doesn't want me around that studio."

"But why?" Susan asked.

Nancy told them of her latest conclusion about the man who had peered in the window. "If he *was* Rugby, I'm going to find out!" she said determinedly.

"He's dangerous!" Bess exclaimed. "Oh, Nancy, don't go to the studio."

Susan spoke up. "I think Bess is right. If he's the kind of person you think he is, you'd better cancel your appointment."

Nancy said she did not want to miss this opportunity to ferret out the facts. "I'll be perfectly safe with Mr. Bradshaw there. I promise you all that if he leaves the studio for long, I'll come home."

Since it had been a busy day, the girls were glad to retire early. The next morning Nancy took her cousin's car and set off for Waverly, the paper footprint in her purse. Bess and George were going to play golf with Susan.

When Nancy reached the studio, both Mr. Bradshaw and his assistant were there. Rugby barely nodded to her and went on with his work. He was cutting glass at a bench.

"Good morning, Nancy," Mr. Bradshaw said

cheerily. "I've been thinking that the best way for you to start learning the window process would be to make a few sketches—any kind you wish. Then I'll tell you whether or not they would divide up well for leading."

He led Nancy to a drawing board, gave her a smock, paper, and some crayons. Then he went back to his own work.

Nancy sat lost in thought for several minutes, then drew a sketch of her dog Togo. She used a background of flowering azaleas and forsythia. Not satisfied with the sketch, she next tried a religious subject. In all she made five before calling Mr. Bradshaw.

"I'm ready," she said.

All this time Nancy had been aware that Alonzo Rugby had been watching her covertly. He had continually found excuses to leave his workbench and glance at Nancy's sketches. Several times it seemed to her as if he wanted to say something but had thought better of it and gone back to his work.

Mr. Bradshaw now came and looked at the various pictures she had made. "You do have talent," he said, smiling. "I especially like the picture of the little dog. Is he yours?"

Nancy nodded. Mr. Bradshaw finally remarked that while it would not be impossible to make stained-glass windows from any of the sketches, none of them was exactly right for the best leading process.

"When using human figures," he said, "it is advisable to show them in an upright position. Or, if they're leaning over, they must be seen in profile. The same applies to animals. Your picture of the dog is very appealing, but with the light coming through a window, his figure would look foreshortened."

Nancy thanked the artist for his constructive comments. "I'll make a few more sketches," she said.

A banjo clock on the studio wall had just chimed eleven thirty when Nancy finished her next one. She had drawn a peacock, its fan spread wide open. She felt that if Mr. Bradshaw and Rugby saw it, possibly one or the other of them would give a hint of any unusual interest they might have in the Greystone window. On impulse, Nancy had made the peacock the size she thought the bird on the shield might be.

"It's pretty good, even if I say so myself," the young sleuth thought.

As she gazed at it, wondering if she should call Mr. Bradshaw over, the artist suddenly stood up. He announced that he was going outside to look for a flower of a certain shade of blue to use in a window. "I'll be right back," he said.

Nancy wondered if Alonzo might follow and

fervently hoped so. Then she could compare his shoe with the paper pattern.

But she was disappointed. The assistant did get up, but instead of going out the door, he turned and came directly to Nancy's drawing board.

"How do you like it?" she asked casually.

Alonzo snorted. "Pretty bad," he said. "You ought to be ashamed of yourself taking up Mr. Bradshaw's time. Anyone can see that you're no artist. Where did you get the idea you were?"

Nancy was stunned for a moment by his sharp criticism. She decided, however, that he was still trying to discourage her from coming to the studio.

Aloud she said, "I'll see what Mr. Bradshaw has to say about it."

Alonzo Rugby's eyes blazed. Before Nancy could stop him, he grabbed the sketch off the drawing board, crumpled it into a tight wad, and threw it with great force across the room. It landed in the fireplace among ashes and half-burned logs!

CHAPTER XI

Surprise Visitors

"Why, how dare you!" Nancy cried out, realizing her sketch was ruined. "You had no right to do that!"

"Yes, I did," Rugby said defiantly, his eyes snapping. "If you haven't got sense enough to get out of here, then I'm the one to see you do!"

Nancy now pretended to be very angry and stalked about the studio. Actually a sense of elation had come over her. She felt that Rugby's sudden rage had probably been caused by the sight of her peacock drawing.

"It could even mean he thinks I know more than I do about the missing window!" she mused.

Keeping up her pretense, Nancy acted as though she were calming down, "Maybe you're right, Mr. Rugby. Suppose you show me some of your sketches which are well suited for stained-glass windows." Secretly she hoped that from them she might pick up a clue to justify her suspicions.

"Very well," Rugby replied haughtily. "But it won't help you any in making sketches yourself. Either you're born with talent or you're not," he added sarcastically.

He showed Nancy a whole portfolio of his drawings, all of which seemed mediocre to her. Apparently Mr. Bradshaw had engaged Rugby to help with the mechanical part of stained-glass windowmaking.

After seeing all the assistant's pictures, Nancy felt disappointed. There were no sketches of knights, horses, shields, or peacocks among them.

"Thank you," said Nancy. "I'll try one more sketch before lunchtime."

As she went back to her drawing board, Mr. Bradshaw returned with several delphinium of various shades of blue. He held them up for Nancy to see.

"They're gorgeous," she said.

"The window I'm working on," Mr. Bradshaw told her, "will have a garden of these pictured."

For the next half hour only the ticking of the clock could be heard as the three artists worked assiduously.

By that time Nancy had a new sketch finished. It portrayed Susan Carr in her beautiful rose garden.

Mr. Bradshaw arose and came over to look at it. He smiled broadly. "Now you've caught on, Nancy. That is excellent," he said. "It has design, character, and good line structure, yet it is simple enough to make a good stained-glass window."

Out of the corner of her eye, Nancy looked at Alonzo Rugby. His face was scarlet, and he was casting angry glances in her direction.

"I'm so glad you like it," Nancy said, a lilt in her voice as if saying to Rugby, "See, you don't know what you're talking about."

Mr. Bradshaw went on, "The woman in this picture looks like Susan Carr. Is it?"

Nancy was thrilled to learn that her sketch was that good. She replied, "Yes," and added excitedly, "Do you suppose you could help me make a small stained-glass window from this? I'd like to give it to my cousin."

"Indeed I do think so," the artist replied. "We'll start on your next lesson tomorrow morning. I guess we'll have to close up shop now. I have a business appointment in town."

Alonzo Rugby took off his lightweight slippers, tucked them into his coat pocket, and put on his shoes. Nancy gave a sigh. There was to be no chance of her comparing either pair of his shoes with the paper pattern of the footprint in the Carr garden.

They all went out and Mr. Bradshaw locked

the door of the studio. Alonzo Rugby said good-by and strode off toward the road. Instead of staying on the gravel path, he stepped onto a little patch of soft earth bordering the driveway. Rugby left perfect imprints of his shoes!

Nancy smiled with satisfaction. The footprints would provide just as good a clue as the man's shoe. Since she did not want Mr. Bradshaw to know yet of her suspicions about his assistant, Nancy decided she could not work while he was around.

"I'll come back here after dark," she told herself, "and compare the left footprint with my pattern."

It occurred to Nancy that she had better leave something which she could pretend to be searching for, in case anyone should find her there. As she walked toward the car with Mr. Bradshaw, Nancy unobtrusively opened her handbag and took out a compact. When Mr. Bradshaw was not looking, she dropped it into some bushes.

"Good-by until tomorrow," the young sleuth said to him, climbing into the car.

At Seven Oaks Nancy was eagerly questioned by Susan, Bess, and George as to how she had made out with her sketching and sleuthing. Quickly she told them what had happened.

"And tonight I'll go back there—to pick up my compact," she said with a chuckle.

The other three girls exchanged glances.

Then Bess, dimpling, said, "You'll have an unexpected escort, Nancy."

"What do you mean, Bess?"

Her friend explained that soon after Nancy
had left, a telephone call had come from Ned
Nickerson. He was just leaving Emerson University with Burt Eddleton and Dave Evans,
friends of George and Bess. The three football
players were on their way to Charlottesville for
an annual college conference.

Nancy smiled delightedly. "That's wonderful. And you mean the boys are coming out
here this evening?"

George nodded. "Susan has invited them to
dinner. If you really have to go sleuthing tonight, Nancy," she added, winking at the others,
"I'm sure Ned won't let you go alone."

"And I wouldn't want him to," said Nancy,
grinning broadly.

When dressing for dinner later, she put on a
becoming, dark-blue cotton dress and soft-soled,
flat-heeled shoes. Nancy figured that in this at-
tire she could not easily be seen or heard while
on her sleuthing mission later in the evening.

At seven o'clock the three boys arrived in a
taxi. Susan, who had never met any of them,
peeked through a window as they came toward the
front door.

"Emerson's finest, I'd say," she remarked with
a chuckle.

"That's Ned in the lead," Nancy told her. Ned was tall, broad-shouldered, and he had brown eyes and hair.

Dave Evans, who dated Bess, was behind Ned. The young man had a rangy build, dark hair, and flashing green eyes. George's favorite escort, Burt Eddleton, was blond. He was a little shorter and heavier than the other two. All three boys were dressed in good-looking sports clothes.

The girls ran out the front door to greet the new arrivals. "Hi!" "Hello!" "How are you?"

Ned took Nancy aside for a moment and whispered in her ear, "Miss me?"

"Sure have," she said, and added facetiously, "but I've been keeping myself busy with Mark Bradshaw."

"Who's he?" Ned demanded.

Nancy teasingly replied that she would explain later.

The boys followed their dates into the house and Nancy presented them to Susan, then to Cliff, who had just come into the living room.

"Good to meet you all," he said.

At dinner the conversation ranged from football to mysteries. Cliff was very much interested in Emerson University's football schedule and said he hoped the team might come down there to play.

"If it does," said Susan, "the girls must come. We'll have a house party for this whole group."

"Why, Sue," said Cliff, laughing, "don't you know these football men will be eating plain, nourishing food at a training table? Beulah's meals would break all diet rules!"

There was light chatter until the end of the meal, then Ned asked for a complete explanation of the mystery Nancy was trying to solve.

"Mysteries, you mean," George corrected.

The boys were astounded to hear all that had happened. Ned was relieved to learn who Mark Bradshaw was, but he was greatly concerned upon hearing that Nancy had been knocked out.

"I wish I could stay around here long enough to find that scoundrel," he said.

"Yes," Burt added, "but we have to leave after the meeting tomorrow."

George's eyes twinkled. "What do you think Bess and I came along for?" she asked. She jokingly flexed the muscles in one of her slim arms. "I'm no weakling!" she remarked.

Ned laughed. "I hate to put you to all that trouble." Then, becoming serious, he asked if there were something he could do that very evening to track down the villain. Nancy told him what she had in mind.

"Perfect," he said. "When do we start?"

Nancy felt they should not begin their investigation until the Bradshaws' house was dark. "Let's go about eleven o'clock," she suggested. "They probably will be asleep by then."

Shortly before eleven, she and Ned started out in the convertible. The moon would not rise until late, but the stars were shining brilliantly. Ned parked some distance beyond the Bradshaws' driveway. Then he took hold of Nancy's arm and the couple walked quietly on the grass along the driveway.

They passed the house without seeing anyone and went on toward the studio. About three hundred feet from it, Nancy whispered:

"I suggest that you wait here for me, Ned. I'm trying to keep my sleuthing a secret. If Mr. Bradshaw or Alonzo Rugby should notice a strange man's footprints alongside mine, they might question me."

Ned agreed and stopped to wait for her in the shadow of some tall bushes. Nancy tiptoed across the driveway and continued on to the studio. The young detective was just about to take her flashlight and paper pattern of the footprint from her bag when she suddenly became aware of a figure inside the studio.

At that instant the door opened and a flashlight was directed at Nancy!

CHAPTER XII

A Dangerous Tackle

As THE door squeaked open, Nancy dodged behind the building and by a fraction of a second avoided detection. She heard the door close and footsteps inside.

For an instant Nancy was tempted to run back and get Ned. Then she realized that the intruder in the studio might leave and she would not be able to find out who he was. Cautiously she moved up to one of the windows.

"It must be an intruder," Nancy reasoned, wondering what to do if she were right.

By the time she reached the window, the light inside had been extinguished. Her heart pounding, she waited. For several seconds all was silent and dark.

"One of us will have to make the first move, I suppose," Nancy told herself.

Just then the light inside the studio beamed

on again.   Nancy looked through the window.
At sight of the intruder she gasped.

Alonzo Rugby!

"What in the world is he doing here at this
time of night?" Nancy asked herself.

As she watched the man moving about fur-
tively, she became convinced that Rugby was not
there with Mr. Bradshaw's knowledge or permission.   Otherwise, his assistant would have turned
on the studio lights.

Suddenly Rugby paused before the fireplace.
Then he leaned down and reached inside.   A
moment later he stood up, a crumpled paper in
his hand.

"The sketch of the peacock I made this morning!" Nancy told herself.   She was so amazed she
could hardly keep from exclaiming aloud.

Rugby laid his flashlight on the floor, then got
down on his hands and knees to smooth out the
drawing.   He went to get a roller from a workbench, and used it on the crumpled sheet.   Then,
sitting back on his heels, the man studied the
drawing.

"Why is he so interested in my sketch?" she
mused.   "If Alonzo doesn't think the drawing is
any good, why is he studying it so closely?"

The man remained on his knees for nearly
five minutes.   Then he picked up the drawing
and slipped it into his portfolio which stood alongside the workbench he used.

As Rugby came toward the door, carrying the portfolio under his arm, Nancy wondered which direction he would take. "If he came in a car," she thought, "he must have parked it still farther up the road from where we left ours."

As Nancy hid among some bushes she wished she might warn Ned. But there was no opportunity to do so. She only hoped that Rugby would not catch her friend off guard.

The assistant came from the studio and locked the door. Then, to Nancy's amazement, he turned toward the woods which lay to the left of the studio.

"I'd certainly like to know where he's going," Nancy thought.

She crept quietly along behind the man. This was not difficult because the path among the trees was fairly smooth and Rugby's flashlight, which he held close to the ground, was powerful enough to light her way. She kept a reasonable distance behind the man who did not turn once.

"I hope this means he doesn't know I'm following him," she thought.

Presently the path forked. Rugby took the right-hand turn and in a few minutes reached the bank of Eddy Run. Setting down the portfolio, he paused a moment on the gravelly shore to light a cigarette. A moment later he shoved a canoe, which was beached there, into the water and stepped in.

Laying the portfolio carefully on the bottom of the canoe, Rugby picked up a paddle and set off upstream in a direction toward Ivy Hall and Cumberland Manor.

"He must live up there somewhere," Nancy told herself as she turned back.

Clicking on her own flashlight, Nancy started back through the woods. Recalling that she had come to Waverly to compare Rugby's footprints with her paper model, she looked for a clear impression of them. At the intersection of the two paths she found a deep one.

"Perfect!" she thought.

Taking the model from her handbag she got down on her hands and knees and laid the paper in the left print.

"It's the same length and width!" she exclaimed elatedly.

Nancy realized that it would be pretty difficult, however, to identify a suspect from just a shoe size. Unfortunately, there were no distinctive marks on the soles or heels of the shoes Rugby had been wearing this evening. In contrast, the pair worn by the man who had pitched the stone had contained a small circle in the center of the heel.

"Just the same, I believe that person was Alonzo Rugby," Nancy concluded. "And I'm going to find out all I can about him to prove either his guilt or his innocence!"

"Ned! Watch out!" Nancy begged

The young sleuth had just made this decision when the stillness was shattered by the loud and unfriendly barking of a dog. In a moment it became evident to Nancy that it was searching for her. The dog began to growl and yap.

She was worried, and instantly began to run. Realizing she could not outdistance the dog, Nancy decided to take refuge in a tree.

Beaming her light around, she chose a young, medium-sized oak and quickly shinned up. She reached the first limb just in the nick of time. A large Doberman pinscher bounded into view. He jumped up angrily, pawing the tree.

"Go home! Shoo!" Nancy commanded, shining her light directly into the dog's eyes and hoping to frighten him away.

But the pinscher had no intention of deserting his prisoner. Nearly five minutes went by. The dog not only showed no signs of leaving, but growled continually.

As Nancy wondered how long she might have to stay in the tree, she realized that her sleuthing had certainly put her in an awkard position.

"I'm literally treed!" she murmured ruefully.

The dog stopped growling for a few seconds. It was long enough, however, to enable Nancy to hear approaching footsteps. Someone was running in her direction.

"This beast's owner, no doubt," Nancy decided.

The pinscher, intent on his quarry, apparently was not aware that someone was coming. Wondering why the person did not have a light, Nancy flashed her own as a guide. A moment later a young man appeared.

Ned Nickerson!

"Look out!" she exclaimed in warning.

At the same moment, the pinscher noticed Ned. With a growl he lunged at him. But the football player side-stepped the dog neatly. Then, with a grip of steel, he grasped the animal by the collar with one hand.

Round and round the two went, the dog trying desperately to shake off his captor. Failing in this, he snapped and yelped, trying his best to bite Ned.

"Watch out!" Nancy begged.

Suddenly, above the sounds of the growling dog, came a man's icy command. "Stop that, Prince!" To Ned, he cried out, "And you ruffian, what are you doing here?"

CHAPTER XIII

The Haunted House

THE speaker, carrying a flashlight, strode into view. Nancy nearly tumbled from her perch in dismay.

The man was Mark Bradshaw!

His mouth set grimly, he stared at Ned, who still held the dog by the collar. An involuntary gasp from Nancy made the artist look up suddenly into the tree. He blinked, then asked:

"What is the meaning of this, Miss Drew?"

As he spoke, Mr. Bradshaw took his pinscher from Ned. The animal immediately quieted down and crouched at his master's feet.

"Mr. Bradshaw," Nancy began, "I'm dreadfully sorry. Before I explain, let me introduce my friend Ned Nickerson. Ned, this is Mr. Bradshaw, the artist who makes stained-glass windows."

Mr. Bradshaw acknowledged the introduction but did not put out his hand to shake Ned's proffered hand.

Nancy hurried on with her explanation. "I know we're trespassing on your property," she said. "I dropped a compact near the studio this morning and returned to get it. Your dog came after me and I ran. I couldn't think of anything else to do but climb a tree. Ned was waiting for me some distance back. When I didn't return, he came to look for me. It's as simple as that, Mr. Bradshaw."

"That's right," Ned spoke up. He thought the man was unnecessarily stern.

Nancy thought so too. "If you don't mind," she said, "I'd like to come down. Will you please hold your dog?"

The artist did not reply to her question. He did speak to the pinscher, though, telling him everything was all right and to be quiet. Nancy shinned down the tree and stood before Mr. Bradshaw.

"Please forgive me," she said. "I'm sorry to have bothered you. Ned and I will hurry along now and I'll see you in the morning."

Mr. Bradshaw did not relax his harsh expression. In icy tones he said, "We'll forget the whole incident, Miss Drew. But I shall be busy for the next few days and unable to give you further lessons."

"Please call me," Nancy requested, but she felt sure this was a permanent dismissal.

The young sleuth berated herself for having been caught. She probably had lost her opportunity to keep an eye on Rugby at the studio.

As she and Ned made their way back toward the driveway, Mr. Bradshaw and the dog followed them. Nancy kept flashing her light as if looking for the compact. When they reached the studio, she saw it, gleaming in the bush. Nancy pounced upon it eagerly, hoping that her action might soften Mr. Bradshaw's attitude. Now, believing that she had told the truth, he might consent to her resuming lessons. But the man continued to walk with them as far as his home without speaking.

"Nice sociable guy," Ned commented a moment later.

Nancy sighed. "He may have heard that I like to solve mysteries and is wondering why I was spying around his place."

When Nancy and Ned reached the Carr home, they heard music and singing. George was doing a comic impersonation. But she stopped in the middle of it and stared at her chum.

"Nancy! Your dress! You look as if you'd been climbing trees."

"I have," Nancy replied with a wry smile, and explained about her predicament.

Instead of sympathizing with Nancy, her

friends burst into laughter. Burt struck a pose as if holding a newspaper and began reading an imaginary headline:

NANCY DREW, GREAT DETECTIVE
TREED BY VILLAINOUS HOUND!

Then he went on to make up a hilarious story while his audience laughed convulsively. Finally, Bess began to feel sorry for Nancy. She knew the young detective deplored having lost her chance to continue sleuthing at the studio.

"Stop your teasing!" she commanded the others. "Let's continue our game of imitating famous people."

Nancy changed her clothes and joined the group. She received a lot of applause for her impersonation of Helena Hawley, a motion-picture star who played parts in old-time westerns.

"You've missed your calling," Cliff declared.

At one o'clock the visiting boys announced they must say good-by. "But we'll see you at Emerson for the Spring Dance."

"We'll be there," the girls chorused.

The following morning, when Nancy was relaxing under a large oak tree wondering how she might find out more about Alonzo Rugby, the rural delivery mailman drove up in his car. Nancy hurried to the letter box at the end of the driveway and reached it before the man finished putting in all the mail.

"Good morning," she said. "I hope there's some out-of-town mail for me."

"If you're Miss Nancy Drew and you're expecting a letter from River Heights, I've brought it," he said cheerfully. When Nancy introduced herself and received the letter, the mailman added, "You know, I deliver a good many letters from River Heights."

Instantly Nancy was on the alert. Recalling Mrs. Dondo and the presumably lost letter from her brother, she asked impulsively, "You mean to Alonzo Rugby?"

"Yes. You know him? I think the letters are from his sister."

"Oh, yes—Mrs. Dondo is a neighbor of mine in River Heights," Nancy remarked, hoping to interest the mailman in saying more.

Her plan succeeded. In the ensuing conversation she learned that Rugby lived on a small farm on Uplands Road.

"He just boards there," said the friendly mailman. "The place is owned by a widow. Her name's Mrs. Paget."

The letter carrier now said good-by and drove off. Nancy stood lost in thought for a moment. She had driven along Uplands Road the previous day. Not only was it nowhere near Eddy Run, but Mrs. Paget's farm was in the opposite direction from that which Rugby had taken in the canoe the evening before.

"Where was he going at that hour?" Nancy mused. "Maybe I can find out from Mrs. Paget!"

Opening her letter, which was from Mr. Drew, Nancy was delighted to hear that Mrs. Dondo had stopped gossiping to the neighbors about her. But she insisted upon prosecuting Mr. Ritter to try to get her hundred dollars. Mr. Drew stated that if his daughter could unearth any clues in Charlottesville, it would help a great deal.

Hurrying to the house, Nancy delivered several letters to the others. Then she told them what her father had written and how she had learned where Rugby lived.

"I'm going over there at the first opportunity," she said.

Nancy knew it would not be possible to go that day because Susan was having the promised party early that evening and needed her car for several errands. Cliff had already left in his.

"We ought to help with the party, anyway," Nancy said to Bess and George.

At luncheon Cliff grinningly made an announcement. "You girls have turned me into a detective. Nancy dropped a hint the other day and I thought I'd take over."

"What is it?" she asked.

"Do you remember telling me you were going to see if any Greystones ever lived in this area? Well, I did it for you."

"Oh, thank you, Cliff. What's the answer?"

Cliff said that he had contacted a historical authority of the area who said there had not been any Greystones from England around the Charlottesville locale in 1850.

"So I'm afraid, Nancy, you're not going to find your stained-glass window here," Cliff said. "But don't be too disappointed."

Nancy laughed. "I'm not giving up yet!"

The Carrs' guests were due to arrive about seven o'clock that evening. Nancy was the first of the three girls to finish dressing. She had put on the lovely pale-green linen. After a final glance in the mirror, she left her room to go downstairs. Passing Susan and Cliff's bedroom she overheard Susan say:

"Alicia Bradshaw phoned, Cliff, and said that she and Mark would not be able to come this evening. She gave no reason. Do you suppose it could be because of what happened last night to Nancy?"

Cliff said something in a low voice and, blushing uncomfortably, Nancy went on downstairs. The last thing she wanted to do was cause any difficulty between Susan and her friends! For a moment she even toyed with the idea of going home, but thought better of it immediately.

"If the Bradshaws are staying away because of me, I think they're acting very strangely."

Nancy forgot the episode when the Carrs and Bess and George joined her a few minutes later.

Soon the guests began to arrive. The girls from River Heights found them all delightful people.

Before long, a good-looking young man named Paul Staunton sought out Nancy. He proved to be a most enjoyable companion and the time flew by. When supper was announced, Paul asked if he might escort her to the buffet table.

"Why, yes, thank you," Nancy replied.

Paul's wish to talk to Nancy alone as they sat together on the patio to eat was shattered.

"Oh, good night," he said, as they noticed a woman approaching. "Here comes that actress, Sheila Patterson. She'll take over the conversation!"

Nancy smiled. When she had met the forty-year-old widow earlier, the girl had found her effusive. The attractive woman had insisted at once that Nancy call her by her first name. Sheila had said she was completely worn out. She was not in a play at the moment but resting at Ivy Hall, an estate which she had recently purchased. Nancy recalled it as the overgrown place she had seen not far from Bradshaw's.

Now, reaching Nancy and Paul, Sheila said dramatically, "Nancy, darling, I've just learned that you're simply marvelous at solving mysteries. I'm so glad I met you. I have a devastating one for you to solve."

Nancy's eyes lighted up. "What is it, Sheila?" she asked the excited actress.

Of medium height and slender build, Sheila had coal-black hair with a dramatic white streak in the front. Her face was youthful, with winged eyebrows which gave her an inquisitive look.

"It's about Ivy Hall," the actress replied, sighing and putting one hand against her temple. "I adored the place at first, but now it has become horribly spooky. All kinds of queer things happen. My daughter Annette and I hear ghostly footsteps at night and a peacock has appeared on our lawn several times."

"A peacock!" Paul laughed, but Nancy tensed.

Sheila stopped speaking and gave a little shudder. Ignoring Paul, she leaned close to Nancy and touched the girl's arm with her cool, slender fingers.

In a strange, tremulous voice, Sheila said, "Nancy, do you know what *peacocks* means to an actress?"

CHAPTER XIV

Spirit Charms

STRANGE noises—ghostly footsteps—peacocks! At once Nancy was intrigued by Ivy Hall.

Recalling that Sheila Patterson had just asked her a question, Nancy said, "I've never heard what peacocks mean to an actress!"

"Well, I'll tell you!" Sheila cried out dramatically. "They bring bad luck—disaster! No actor or actress in his right mind will appear on the stage if there's a peacock, real or artificial, anywhere around."

The woman flung her arms above her head, then buried her face in her hands. "That peacock on my lawn! I know what it means. I'll never get another part in a play!"

Despite the fact that she felt the woman was exaggerating her fear, Nancy felt genuinely sorry for her. She had often met persons who had let superstitions affect their lives, but Nancy was astounded that a person of Sheila's talents and intelligence could believe such an absurd thing. Taking hold of the actress's hand, Nancy asked her to sit down and talk it over.

Paul Staunton had been standing all this time. Now he said, "Perhaps you two would like to be alone. I'll be back later, Nancy."

Nancy flashed him an understanding smile, then turned to Sheila. "Please try not to be upset about the mystery at your home. You know, most people believe that peacocks bring good luck, not bad luck."

"No, I never heard that," Sheila answered absently, calming down a bit. But she started to twist a lace handkerchief nervously. Looking pleadingly into Nancy's eyes, she said, "It would give me a lot of hope and confidence if you'd come over to Ivy Hall for a few days. Maybe I'm foolish, but until I find out there's nothing supernatural going on, I must believe that there's only bad luck in store for me."

"I'd like to come," said Nancy thoughtfully, "if—"

"Yes?"

The young sleuth said she had come south with her friends Bess and George. If Nancy went to Ivy Hall, she would want them to accompany her. Also, since they were Susan's guests, she must first speak to her cousin.

"Oh, I intended that your two friends should

come," Sheila said warmly, "and I know Susan won't mind." She suddenly hugged Nancy and gave her a butterfly kiss on the cheek. "You're a darling—a perfect darling! Come tomorrow. I can't stand it much longer with just Annette and me there. I'd move, but I've put all my money into the place. Oh, the whole thing's dreadful! My nerves are nearly shattered!"

At that moment her daughter Annette came up and put her arms around her mother's neck. The girl appeared to be about eighteen years old, had beautiful curly auburn hair and a cute tilted-up nose. Small-boned, she walked and moved in a quick, elfinlike manner. After speaking to Nancy, she said:

"Mother dear, I think perhaps we'd better go. You're becoming too excited."

"Oh, I'm all right now," Sheila said, looking at her daughter affectionately. "And what do you think, my love? Nancy Drew and her friends are coming over to stay with us and solve our mystery!"

"We'll try, anyway," Nancy said, smiling.

Annette Patterson looked relieved. "Well, I'm glad to hear that. Thanks a million. But I must say, Nancy, that you have courage!"

Nancy said that if Susan had not made plans for her for the next two days, she and her friends would be at Ivy Hall in the morning.

"Thanks, darling." Sheila hugged Nancy again.

As soon as the Pattersons moved off, Paul Staunton returned with fresh plates of warm food, and he and Nancy spent the rest of the evening together. After all the guests had left, the Carrs sat down with their visitors for a chat.

"The party was super," said George.

"Dreamy," was Bess's comment.

Nancy mentioned what a delightful time she had had, and also how much she had enjoyed the Carrs' friends.

"And they all liked you girls," Susan said. With a chuckle she glanced at Nancy and added, "Particularly Paul Staunton."

Nancy blushed. "He's a lot of fun."

"I noticed," said Cliff, "that Sheila had you cornered. "What were you talking about?"

Nancy told the group of Sheila's invitation, then asked Susan if she would mind their accepting.

"Go ahead, by all means. But don't forget Garden Week. We have some dates, you know."

Cliff spoke up. "How about Cumberland Manor, Nancy? Have you given up trying to persuade Mr. Honsho to open it for us?"

"No, indeed. As a matter of fact, it's because there may be a peacock in each place that I'm going to Ivy Hall. Maybe, just maybe, there's a connection!"

"That's right," Cliff agreed. "Nancy, you amaze me."

Susan offered the use of her car, telling Nancy to keep it as long as she wished.

Bess sighed. "I was almost hoping you'd object," she said. "Ugh! Ghosts and peacocks!"

The three girls packed their suitcases before going to bed and were up early the next morning. Coming down to breakfast, they found Beulah wringing her hands and tossing her head from side to side. Susan explained that the cook was fearful of the girls' planned visit to the Pattersons'.

"Indeed I am," Beulah said. Rolling her eyes around, she added, "Ivy Hall's always been haunted—from way back. You're takin' your life in your hands to go there."

Nothing Nancy could say would persuade the maid that there was no such thing as a ghost. Finally, Beulah sighed and reached into the pocket of her apron. She handed Bess a rabbit's foot, George an elephant's tooth, and Nancy a little vial which she said contained ground up toads.

"You all better sleep with these under your pillows," she advised.

The girls thanked Beulah and managed to suppress smiles of amusement.

Beulah went on to explain the value of these "charms." "They'll help to ward off the ghosts," she said. "Oh, Miss Nancy, I wish you and Miss Bess and Miss George weren't goin'. But if there's no talkin' you out of it, Lord bless you all and take care of you!"

Nancy said it was very kind of Beulah to be so concerned. At ten o'clock the girls set off for Ivy Hall. On reaching the entrance to the untended, overgrown estate, Nancy turned in and drove up to the colonial red-brick house, the sides of which were thickly covered with ivy. It had an impressive front porch with majestic white columns.

On the steps stood Annette Patterson and a young man. The girl was shaking her head vigorously and looked annoyed.

"Well, what do you know!" Bess exclaimed. "That's the same 'cowboy' we saw at Cumberland Manor—the one who wouldn't talk to us!"

Just then the "cowboy" jumped on his bicycle, which had been lying against the steps, and pedaled quickly down the driveway.

"We'll ask Annette about him later," Nancy remarked, as the girls alighted from the car.

Annette, who was wearing pink Bermuda shorts and a candy-striped blouse, ran toward the girls with a happy "Hi!" Then Sheila, similarly attired, came hurrying from the hall. Being more effusive than her daughter, she planted resounding kisses on the cheeks of her visitors.

"You are lambs to come!" Sheila cried gaily, hooking one arm into Nancy's and leading the girls into the house. "Isn't this a heavenly place?" she asked.

"Yes, it's charming," replied Nancy, admiring the large center hall with its graceful, wide stairway.

"Let's take the girls on a tour of inspection, Mother," Annette said enthusiastically.

Sheila led the way first into the living room to the left of the hallway, then the dining room on the right. They were sunny and spacious, but draperies and wallpaper were faded and in places badly torn. The chairs and tables were sadly in need of repair.

"I bought the house furnished," Sheila said quickly, "and intend to renovate when I can. But for now—" She shrugged, then went on, "Annette and I have always lived in hotels until recently."

"But never again, I hope!" Annette said fervently. "I love Ivy Hall and never want to leave it."

"Unless we're forced to," her mother said sadly.

"I'm sure you'll be able to stay," Nancy spoke up.

French doors at the end of the living room led to a walnut-paneled library practically bare of furniture. Bess glanced at its bookless shelves and shuddered inwardly. The room, a dark one, had an eerie appearance.

Sheila hurried her guests out of it, led them through a modern pantry and kitchen, then onto a screened-in porch off the dining room. Here, she said, they spent a great deal of time in mild weather.

"I would too," Nancy commented, glancing at the comfortable glider.

Annette pointed out the old slave quarters a hundred and fifty feet away, now tumble-down and covered with ivy. "That's where all the cooking was done in the olden days," she explained.

"How romantic!" Bess murmured.

Sheila sighed. "My gardens are dreadful, because we have no help. I put every cent we could spare into buying this place, and the upkeep—" She stopped speaking. Apparently a thought she did not want to express aloud had come to her.

"Mother and I are sort of camping out here," Annette said in her direct way. "Even if we could afford it, I doubt that we could find servants willing to come here. We had one and she spread talk of the house being haunted." Then she added, "I hope you girls don't mind having simple meals."

"Oh, we'll be glad to help," Bess spoke up.

George laughed. "If you make Bess chief cook you can be sure of always having a real feast."

Next, Sheila and Annette showed the girls the rambling second floor of Ivy Hall, with its six bedrooms and two baths. Undoubtedly it, too, had once been very beautiful, but now needed restoration. The mahogany woodwork was nicked and the long hall carpet threadbare.

"This will be your bedroom," Sheila told the girls, opening a paneled door. "It overlooks the old slave quarters."

The room was large, its windows adorned with faded but lovely damask draperies. A huge canopied mahogany bed and a cot with a flowered quilt stood along one wall. The other furniture was simple.

After lunch Nancy, Bess, and George unpacked, and spent the rest of the day with Annette wandering around the estate. Nancy was particularly interested in a closed stairway at the end of the second-floor hall. It led to the attic.

"It may come in handy to know about this," she said half-jokingly, winking at George.

By suppertime the girls had thoroughly memorized the layout of the house and the grounds.

"I could almost find my way around in the dark," Nancy said, but Sheila said this would not be necessary. There were electric lights everywhere except in the attic.

When the visitors said good night at ten o'clock and went upstairs, Annette followed them into their room and sat down to chat. She asked about River Heights and the girls' friends. Nancy described their home town briefly, and Bess spoke enthusiastically of Ned, Burt, and Dave. Then

Nancy mentioned the young man she had seen on the Pattersons' porch that morning.

"Is he someone you date?" she asked Annette.

The girl looked blank for a moment. Then she said, "Oh, you mean Luke Seeny."

Bess giggled. "Is he a real cowboy, Annette?"

"Yes, he is—from Oklahoma. I met him at a dance. Luke's been trying for over a week to date me, but I don't care for him. All he does is brag about his wealthy family back home."

"Where does he stay up here?" Nancy asked.

"At a hotel in Charlottesville."

This information surprised Nancy and her friends, who had expected to hear that Luke lived with Mr. Honsho at Cumberland Manor.

"What is Luke doing in Charlottesville?" George questioned.

"Oh, nothing special, I guess," Annette answered. "Just sightseeing."

The other girls exchanged glances. Luke's story about doing nothing in particular did not ring true, but they did not mention this to Annette. Presently she arose, said good night, and wished them pleasant dreams.

"I wish so, too," said Bess, after Annette had closed the door. "Ivy Hall gives me a funny feeling. It's hard to describe, but even if I hadn't heard that the place is haunted, I'd have guessed it myself."

"Now, Bess," Nancy said with a grin, "you don't mean that!"

George gave her cousin a look of reproach. "You'll sleep sounder than any of us," she prophesied, "and in the morning you'll take back those words."

Bess and George climbed into the canopied bed, since Nancy insisted that she would sleep on the cot. With the lights out, Ivy Hall seemed extremely dark and quiet. There was not a sound in the house and outside only the chirping of crickets could be heard. Soon all three girls were sound asleep.

About midnight Nancy was awakened by sounds of someone moving around in the attic. Listening intently, she could distinctly hear boards creaking overhead.

Bess and George awoke too. There was no doubt but that someone was walking in the attic.

"The ghost!" Bess shrieked.

CHAPTER XV

A Weird Disappearance

"Oh, it's true!" Bess cried out excitedly. "There *are* ghosts in this house." She dived under the covers and lay motionless.

George turned on the night-table lamp and said, "Shame on you, Bess. We came here to help Nancy solve the mystery. Get up! Let's go!"

"You—you tell me about it later," Bess said unhappily.

Nancy was already up and putting on her robe and slippers. George hurriedly donned her own, then determinedly put Bess's slippers on her.

As Nancy turned the doorknob she said quietly, "Never mind, George. The two of us can go."

"Oh, I don't want to be left alone!" Bess cried out. "Wait for me!" She quickly put on her robe and followed Nancy and her cousin into the hall.

Annette, in pajamas, was standing outside her own bedroom, a look of fright on her face. "You heard it, too?" she whispered. In a low voice Nancy said, "We're going up to the attic. Want to come?"

"Oh, you'd better not! Something might happen to you," Annette warned. "I wouldn't dare go, anyway. I promised Mother I never would."

Nancy quietly opened the door to the attic stairway. She looked on the wall for a light switch, then remembered there was none.

"You'll have to use a candle," Annette said.

On a small table in the hallway stood a glass candleholder with a short white candle in it. Annette picked up a packet of matches beside it and with trembling fingers lighted the candle. Nancy, meanwhile, chided herself that she had left her flashlight in the car.

"Here you are," Annette said, handing the candle to Nancy, who went at once to the stairway.

The creaking sounds above had not been repeated. Bess, last in line of the trio, said in a shaky voice:

"The ghost must be hiding!"

The others did not comment. Reaching the top step they looked around cautiously. Several old curved-top trunks stood about, discarded draperies hung on lines, and large paintings in ornate gold frames were propped against the eaves.

Nancy set the candle down on a table in the middle of the room and the three girls began looking back of the various objects to see if anyone were hiding. They found no one. Next, Nancy started to open trunks to determine if the "ghost" were inside. As she lifted back the lid of the third one, Bess gasped and Nancy and George stepped back in horror.

A little girl, her eyes closed, lay in the trunk!

For a moment the three stared horrified. Then suddenly they smiled. The figure was that of a very large lifelike doll!

The rest of the trunks were examined but revealed no one hiding inside.

As Nancy and George stood gazing about the attic, wondering if there were any other entrance, Bess became fascinated by a large painting at one end of the room.

The picture portrayed a dashing cavalier, his waxed mustache perfectly groomed. The man's turned-up hat was worn at a rakish angle, with a feather curled smartly over his shoulder.

The cavalier's eyes seemed to stare at Bess as she walked about. Drawn to it like a magnet, she went to the far side of the attic to take a close look at the gallant gentleman's face. It looked so real that it seemed almost to be alive.

Nancy and George, meanwhile, had been studying the wall on the opposite side of the attic. It was higher than any of the other three unfinished walls and was paneled. The two girls walked toward it to see if there might be a concealed entrance to another room.

Hearing a slight gasp, Bess turned around. To her astonishment, neither of the other girls was in sight.

"Nancy! George! Where are you?" she called.

Bess's heart began to pound. Her friends must have gone downstairs without her!

"I'm not going to stay up here alone," she told herself, and headed for the stairway.

As Bess picked up the candle, she suddenly stopped short in panic. A few feet ahead of her stood a swaying form in white. *The ghost!*

Bess stared at it, too terrified to utter a sound. Suddenly the figure took a step toward her. With a great leap Bess passed it, dashed toward the stairway, and raced down the steps pell-mell, making a terrific clatter.

Annette, hearing her, hurried to the foot of the stairs. One look at Bess's terrified expression convinced her that the girl must have seen something frightening in the attic.

"What was it?" she cried out, taking the candle from Bess's trembling hand.

"A—a—gh-ghost!" Bess wailed and slumped to the floor. Her legs would no longer hold her.

"Then it's true! The house *is* haunted!" Annette cried out.

Bess nodded and in a frantic whisper asked, "Where are Nancy and George?"

"What do you mean?" Annette asked. "Weren't they with you?"

Bess stared in stupefaction. "You—you mean they didn't come d-down here?"

"No."

Bess gave a cry of alarm. "Then they're gone!" she moaned. "The ghost got them!"

The commotion had awakened Sheila Patterson. Now she hurried into the hall in a frilly nightgown. On hearing what had happened, she paced back and forth, waving her arms dramatically and crying out:

Ahead of her stood a swaying form in white.
The ghost!

"Oh, what will we do? What will we do?"

"We could call the police," said Annette.

Bess, though frightened, realized that if Nancy and George were in trouble, she must help them at once. They could not wait for the police!

Bess's courage returned. She stood up and said with determination, "Come on, Annette! We'll have to go back to the attic and rescue the girls!"

Sheila grabbed her daughter's arm. "No, you mustn't go! I won't let you!"

"Mother, we have to do *something!*" Annette urged. "Nancy and George were willing to come here and risk their lives to help us. It's our responsibility if something has happened to them!"

"Oh, I know—I know!" moaned Sheila.

A thought came to Bess. "You know, my cousin sometimes plays tricks on me," she spoke up. "Maybe George found a sheet in the attic and played ghost to scare me!"

Somewhat reassured, Sheila finally agreed to allow her daughter to go up to the attic. As Bess started up the steps, the actress's conscience began to bother her.

"I'm going along," she said.

Bess reached the top and held the candle high. As she paused to look around, a current of air suddenly blew out her light.

Standing almost paralyzed in total darkness, she heard a door somewhere in the old house squeak eerily, then close with a terrific bang!

CHAPTER XVI

The Slave Tunnel

FIFTEEN minutes earlier, Nancy and George had been walking across the attic toward the paneled wall. Without warning, the floor had opened beneath their feet!

The two girls found themselves shooting down a steep wooden slide into pitch blackness. A trap door above them closed quietly. They landed abruptly on a hard surface at the bottom of the chute.

"Oh, my head!" George groaned. "Nancy, are you all right?"

"I guess so. I banged my shoulder a little."

The two girls untangled themselves and slowly stood up. Both groped around and could feel with the tips of their fingers a dank ceiling a few inches above their heads.

"Where do you suppose we are?" George asked.

"In the cellar, probably." Nancy smiled ruefully. "That was a fast ride!"

George heaved a sigh. "Where do we go now?"

Nancy ran her fingers over the slippery surface of the slide. "We never could crawl up that long chute," Nancy replied. "We'll have to try getting out of here some other way."

The girls stood still a few minutes waiting to see if Bess would also shoot down the slide. They braced themselves to catch her. Nancy called up the opening, telling what had happened.

"Turn on the light in the cellar and open the door, will you?" she shouted.

There was no answer. "I suppose," said George, "that when Bess missed us, she got out of the attic in a hurry."

"No doubt. George, what I can't understand is why the trap door opened all of a sudden. I'm sure we walked over it several times before."

George whispered in Nancy's ear, "There's only one answer. That ghost we were trying to find must have opened it."

"Which means," Nancy replied in a low tone, "that he may still be at the top of this slide in a niche. Well, George, we'll have to rescue ourselves. Let's start."

Nancy ran her hands along the ceiling, floor, and side walls. "George, I think we must be in some kind of a tunnel. Maybe it was an old one used by the slaves years ago and led from their quarters to the main house."

"Well, the sooner we get to the end of it, the happier I'll be," George replied. "Let's go!"

The two girls got down on their hands and knees and began to inch their way along the floor, side by side. They felt ahead cautiously before moving forward.

After progressing some twenty-five feet, George said, "This sure is slow work." Her knees began to burn and she was sure most of the skin had been scraped off them.

Fifty feet beyond, the girls came to a heavy door and stood up to examine it. The door had a huge, old-fashioned iron latch and slide bolt, both of which were coated with rust. Though the girls pushed with all their strength to move them, Nancy and George were not able to budge the bolt even a fraction of an inch.

"Dead end!" George remarked woefully.

"I'm afraid so," Nancy answered. "We'll have to go back where we started from and try the other direction."

This time the girls felt it was safe to walk upright. With Nancy on the right and George on the left, they moved fairly rapidly, but each kept one hand on the wall nearest her. By the time they reached the spot where Nancy thought they would find the slide, George was considerably in the lead.

"Wait!" Nancy called. She was about to say

that from this point on they should once more crawl on their hands and knees when George cried out from the pitch blackness:

"Help!"

"What's the matter?" Nancy asked quickly.

There was no response and suddenly Nancy could hear the splashing of water. George must have fallen into a well or pit!

Dropping to her knees, Nancy crawled forward rapidly. In a moment she reached what seemed to be a pool.

"George, where are you? Answer me!" she cried, fear gripping her.

Then, to her intense relief, George replied, "I'm all right but I went down under water. Keep talking, so I can swim toward your voice."

Nancy encouraged George, who said the water was icy cold. A few seconds later the two girls touched hands and Nancy pulled her friend from the underground water hole.

"Thank goodness you're all right!" Nancy exclaimed. "I wonder how wide the water hole is." She feared that any escape this way was cut off.

George said the pit seemed very large to her, but perhaps she was overestimating its size.

"I'll try to find out," said Nancy.

While she began feeling her way along the edge of the water, George remained behind, trying to wring out her soaking wet bathrobe and pajamas. She had lost her slippers in the water.

"This seems to be more like a large well," Nancy reported. "It's only in the center of the tunnel. I think we can creep along the edge safely and get to the other side of the water."

George, dragging her soggy bathrobe behind her, crawled after Nancy. Soon they came to the far side of the big well. For safety, they remained on their knees and proceeded very cautiously. Foot by foot, they went on without coming to the end of the tunnel.

"This must run all the way to Charlottesville," said George disgustedly.

Nancy had a feeling that George's courage was beginning to wane. She herself was growing more concerned about their predicament. Suppose the inside end of the tunnel was blocked also!

To keep up George's spirits as well as her own, Nancy said with a chuckle, "If the slaves had to walk along this bumpy path carrying trays of food, they must have had a lot of spills."

"I'll say," George replied. "Can't you just see a big silver tray with a freshly roasted turkey being dropped upside down on this earthen floor!"

The remark made both girls laugh and each felt better. Suddenly Nancy's outstretched hand touched a wooden step.

"End of the trail!" she said happily as the girls inched their way up the stairs.

The flight was very steep, and at the top Nancy could not feel any doorknob. latch, or lock.

George had no better luck. "The exit has been boarded up!" she said fearfully. "What do we do now?"

Nancy did not reply. Though she feared her friend was right, the young sleuth began to look for a way to slide or rotate a section of the wall. After several tries, her fingertips caught in a narrow crevice and she felt the end of a panel move slightly.

"It's a sliding door, George," Nancy reported excitedly. "Help push!"

Together, the two girls stuck their fingers into the tiny opening and shoved with all their might. The panel began to give, but it squeaked and groaned loudly.

"Spooky!" George remarked, as the girls made an opening wide enough for them to squeeze through.

Nancy and George found themselves in a large closet filled with dishes. At the opposite side was a door with a handle, which opened easily, though the door creaked eerily.

The two girls walked through into the kitchen of Ivy Hall where moonlight streamed through the windows. It was a welcome relief from the total darkness of the tunnel.

"Thank goodness we're free!" George exclaimed.

The closet door swung shut with a tremendous bang which made both Nancy and George jump.

As they proceeded toward the front hall, George remarked:

"The squeaking and the bang have probably scared the Pattersons and Bess out of a year's growth!"

"Unless they're already frightened by our absence," said Nancy. As she started to ascend the stairway, Nancy called loudly, "Bess! Annette! Sheila!"

Instantly footsteps came pounding down the attic steps. In a few moments the whole group had assembled in the second-floor hall.

"Nancy! George!" Bess cried out. "Where have you been? We thought the ghost got you!"

"Not us," her cousin retorted.

Bess pointed. "Look at your night clothes!"

Glancing down, Nancy and George saw how disheveled they were. Their pajamas and robes were streaked with black dirt.

"And, George, you're soaking wet!" Annette cried out.

Despite her discomfort, George could not help laughing. "I've been swimming," she said.

"Tell me, quickly, what happened to you girls!" Sheila demanded.

Nancy and George described their harrowing experience. "I didn't know about the trap door and the tunnel," Sheila said, shivering a little. "Oh, this house is too, too weird!"

When Nancy heard that Bess had really seen a

ghost, her eyes opened wide. This meant that the impersonator could not have been hiding below the trap door after she and George went through it.

Nancy looked at the others questioningly. "Did that ghost come down the attic stairs?" she asked Bess.

"No."

"Well, he didn't follow George and me through the tunnel," she said. "That means he must still be in the house. We're going to find him!"

Sheila Patterson stared in amazement. "How can you find a ghost? It's not real! It can just vanish at will."

Nancy said she was certain that Bess's ghost was a human being. "And I intend to locate him! Come on, everybody!" she urged, and started determinedly up the attic stairs.

CHAPTER XVII

An Attic Discovery

WITH Nancy in the lead holding the candle, the entire group trooped to the attic. Bess almost expected to see the ghost standing near the stairway, but there was no sign of it. The attic apparently was deserted.

"But the ghost, if he is a real person, might be hidden!" Bess said nervously, looking around apprehensively.

"We'll smoke him out!" George said with determination. "But, for goodness sake, don't anybody step on the trap door!"

She pointed out its location. When Nancy held the candle close to the floor, the outline of the trap was plainly visible. The young sleuth got down alongside it and pushed on the door. It would not open!

"That's strange," she remarked. "This trap

door must work by some mechanism we aren't aware of."

Annette suggested that perhaps it took more weight to open the door. The girls pushed a trunk loaded with books over the spot, but still the trap door did not budge.

"Did you touch anything, Nancy, before we took our slide?" George asked.

Nancy shook her head. "But I feel sure there's some secret mechanism in this attic which will open the trap door. I'm going to look for it."

Bess grabbed Nancy's wrist and whispered, "Maybe the ghost is hiding wherever it is! Please be careful, Nancy!"

"I will." The girl detective moved to the paneled wall which had aroused her curiosity earlier. Now she began examining every inch of it. Suddenly Nancy cried out excitedly:

"I think I've found the secret!"

The others crowded around as she silently slid back the whole section of panel. No one was hidden in the small enclosure beyond.

"This is probably where your ghost came from, Bess," said Nancy.

"Sure," George added. "You didn't hear him leave his hide-out because this panel doesn't squeak when it's opening." She gestured toward an open trunk full of linen. "And the ghost used a sheet from that."

Nancy handed the candle to George. "Hold

this and shine the light in here, will you?" she requested.

George did this while Nancy tested the flooring behind the panel. Finding it firm, she stepped inside. On the front wall she found a lever and pushed it.

At once the trap door opened downward!

"Oh!" cried Bess, blinking rapidly.

The Pattersons looked at Nancy in awe. Finally Annette said, "Nancy, you're certainly a genius! Mother and I never would have found the lever!"

George was thoughtful. "I can't understand what the slide is doing there and who put it in."

Nancy thought it might have been used to transfer supplies from the attic to the tunnel. "Perhaps during the Civil War," she added, "Ivy Hall's owner installed it."

After Nancy closed the trap door, she stepped out into the attic. Pulling the panel shut, she suggested that they all go downstairs and get some sleep.

"But where's the ghost?" Bess asked, perplexed. She shivered. "I don't feel like sleeping while he's still around."

"Nor I," Annette admitted.

When they reached the second floor, Nancy put an arm around Bess. "Tell me honestly, honey, were you watching the attic steps every second after you came down here?"

Bess replied that she had not been, nor had Sheila and Annette.

"Then," Nancy deduced, "I believe the masquerader may have followed you down the attic steps, Bess. While you were talking to Sheila and Annette, he probably slipped into the bedroom at the end of the hall, then made his escape to the first floor when the three of you returned to the attic."

Sheila Patterson had said nothing for the past few minutes. Now she began pacing tragically up and down the hall, her nightgown swirling around her lithe figure.

"Things have gone too far around here!" she cried out excitedly. "We may all be murdered in our beds! Girls, we're not staying here another minute. I want everyone to pack immediately. You three girls return to Susan's. Annette and I will go to a hotel!"

The others were shocked by the actress's order. Annette spoke up quickly, "But, Mother, it's the middle of the night. By the time we could pack and get ready to leave, it will be dawn, anyway."

"I don't care *what* time it is!" Sheila burst out, her eyes flashing. "I won't live in a house with a ghost—spook or human—another minute!"

Annette looked unhappy. "I don't blame you, Mother, but to leave now means admitting defeat. If we stick it out, we may find the explanation. Besides, it's our home."

"I'll tell you what," George said sensibly. "Suppose two of us at a time stand guard while the others sleep."

It took the combined efforts of all the girls to persuade the excited actress to remain at least until morning. Finally, Sheila looked at her daughter and said, "All right, baby, we'll see what happens."

Nancy and Bess went on the first watch of two hours, sitting in chairs near the attic entrance. Then George and Annette took over. Morning dawned without anything having happened.

The sunshine of the warm spring day streamed through the windows of Ivy Hall, and everyone felt cheered.

Sheila, having finally had a few hours of unbroken rest, actually began to sing. With the girls' help she prepared a delicious breakfast and they all sat down on the screened-in porch to eat it.

"I'm sorry I became so hysterical last night," she said contritely. "I've been thinking things over calmly, but it still seems to me that it would be foolish for any of us to stay here."

Nancy spoke up quickly. "I believe that's exactly what the ghost is hoping you'll think."

"What do you mean?" the actress asked, puzzled.

Nancy's answer startled everyone. She said the ghost wanted the house vacated immediately. "He thinks something valuable is hidden here and is looking for it. He must be very familiar with the place, since he knows about the trap door. Sheila, if you leave here, the ghost will have the run of the place. You own this property and anything hidden on it is yours. You and Annette might be cheating yourselves out of some valuable object if you move away."

"I suppose we would," the actress conceded. She asked if Nancy had any idea as to what Ivy Hall's treasure might be, and once more confided to the girls that she and Annette were very much in need of cash. "Do you think it might be money?"

"I doubt it," said Nancy. "But I do have one theory regarding what the treasure might be."

She told the Pattersons about the missing stained-glass window and that Sir Richard Greystone was offering a large reward to anyone giving information as to its whereabouts. "That's the real reason Bess and George and I came to Virginia," Nancy confessed.

"How simply fascinating!" Annette exclaimed.

But Sheila looked worried. "You say there's a peacock on the window? Oh, I hope it's not hidden here!"

"Why, Mother," said Annette, "if the window's hidden in Ivy Hall, we might sell it to Sir Richard for a large sum."

"I suppose that's true, dear."

Nancy asked Sheila if any former owner of the

place was named Greystone. The actress could not recall whether any of the old deeds showed that a family by that name had ever lived there.

"And I doubt that the window is hidden here," the actress went on. "Before I purchased Ivy Hall, Annette and I looked at the property carefully. We saw nothing to indicate that a stained-glass window was ever built into any of the walls."

Nancy could not agree. Her mind had been moving swiftly from one possible suspect to another to determine who might be playing ghost. "The most likely," she thought, "is Alonzo Rugby." Aloud the girl detective merely said, "The window may have been taken out and put somewhere. Anyway, why don't we all hunt for a clue to it?"

"Yes, let's!" Annette urged.

As soon as breakfast was over, Sheila and the girls tidied up the kitchen, the porch, and their bedrooms. By ten o'clock they were ready for the search.

Walls, floors, cabinets, and closets were investigated but yielded no clue.

"If the window was removed," said George, "then it may have been taken apart and the pieces packed away. So I'd say it's back to the attic for us!"

Every trunk and box in the third floor was emptied. The girls were fascinated by the old costumes, magazines, sheet music, and other trophies of a bygone era, the accumulation of several generations of inhabitants of Ivy Hall. But no real treasure came to light and not even one piece of stained glass was found.

"I don't like to doubt you, Nancy," said Sheila finally, "but I'm sure there's nothing of real value around here."

"Unless the ghost found it last night and took it with him," Bess spoke up.

Nancy smiled. "In that case," she said, "he won't be back."

This reasoning made Sheila change her mind about moving out at once. She agreed to stay one more night at least.

Nancy was pleased to hear this. She had been on the verge of asking if she and her friends might remain even if the others left. When Sheila suggested that they all relax on the porch with glasses of lemonade, Nancy reminded her that they had not examined the tunnel or the slave quarters.

"I can't, I can't!" Sheila exclaimed. "I'm exhausted now. You girls do it."

Nancy was overruled in declining the cool drink. But as soon as the tall glasses of lemonade had been emptied, she took her flashlight and a wrench from the car, and led the way through the secret door of the dish closet.

When the girls reached the pool into which George had fallen, the tomboy laughed. "It's only a good-sized well," George chided herself. "Probably this was where the slaves stopped to fill pitchers on their way to serve meals."

Nancy stopped at the slide and looked up. Wooden boards had been nailed over a stairway, to convert it to a chute. The tunnel did not contain a single object and soon the searchers reached the end of it.

Using the wrench, Nancy managed to hammer back the rusted bolt. The door creaked open and the girls found themselves in the remains of a kitchen.

"We're in the slave quarters!" Annette exclaimed.

"How quaint!" Bess said dreamily, viewing the huge fireplace and copper kettles hanging on the bricks.

One side of the room, and apparently the rest of the building, had caved in. But in the rubble Nancy caught sight of a discarded ornamental sheet of cast iron. Walking over to it, she threw the light directly on the design. The others crowded around.

"*A peacock!*" Bess cried out. "Where was this used?"

Annette explained that it was a fireback, set in the rear of a fireplace to reflect heat into the room. It probably had been used many years ago in one of the rooms of Ivy Hall.

"Now I'm convinced," said Nancy, "that residents of this house at one time were interested in using peacocks as a design."

"Yes," said Bess, "but it doesn't prove that the stained-glass window was ever here."

Nancy did not comment, but as they started back through the tunnel, she said, "There's one thing I haven't done. That is to look outdoors for footprints of the ghost."

Leaving the others in the kitchen, she went down the back-porch steps and began a systematic search for the prints. Suddenly she saw something which made her gasp in amazement.

At the top of her voice, Nancy cried out, "Come here, everybody!"

CHAPTER XVIII

A Midnight Chase

IMMEDIATELY the Pattersons hurried to Nancy's side, followed by Bess and George. The young sleuth was down on hands and knees outside a basement window which was almost completely hidden by a heavy growth of shrubbery.

"Careful where you walk!" she called out. "Here are some peculiar footprints."

The others followed Nancy's pointing finger. Deeply embedded in the sod and dirt were the prints of a three-toed bird. At once Sheila's face took on a look of alarm. In a trembling voice she asked, "Do they belong to a peacock?"

"Yes and no," Nancy replied ambiguously.

The others waited for her to explain. After making some measurements, she looked up and said, "See these marks. Sometimes they're close together, and at other times far apart."

"What does that prove?" Bess asked.

"It means," said Nancy, "that a human being and not a bird made these marks."

Annette paled. "You—you mean a human being with a bird's feet?" she questioned unbelievingly.

Nancy said that she believed the human being had strapped artificial peacocks' claws to the bottom of his shoes to avoid making footprints that might be recognizable.

Bess asked her if she had any theory who the intruder had been.

"Yes," Nancy replied. "I think it was our ghost friend. And he's more interested in peacocks than we figured. But first, I'd like to prove my theory about these footprints. Let's follow the marks."

The group had no difficulty in doing this. The prints were visible as far as Eddy Run. Here they vanished and there were no imprints of any kind, bird or human, along the shore line.

"Maybe the spook can fly," George quipped.

As the group turned back toward Ivy Hall, Nancy's eyes swept the entire area. Suddenly she dashed off a short distance and picked up an object embedded in the mud. "I've found the answer!" she exclaimed exultantly.

Coming back to the others, Nancy showed them a bronze cast of a peacock's foot with straps attached.

"It must have dropped off the man's shoe," said Nancy. "I presume this bird man came and went in a boat, so there's no chance of following him."

Walking back to the house everyone discussed this new angle of the mystery. But when they reached Ivy Hall, Sheila insisted that all sleuthing cease for the day. "This is the strangest Sunday I ever spent in my life," she said. "I think we all should have a little spiritual uplift!"

"But I don't think," said Annette, "that we should leave the house for long."

Sheila nodded. With dramatic steps she marched to an old-time organ in the parlor, opened it, and began to play hymns. Though it wheezed a bit and some notes did not sound, the girls managed to keep in tune and joined her in singing for over an hour. The religious atmosphere was relaxing and this peaceful mood remained until bedtime. Then Sheila began to worry again.

"I shan't sleep a wink," she said, "unless everything in Ivy Hall is nailed tight shut. There seem to be all kinds of entrances to this old house that we don't find ourselves but other people use. The ghost must have come through that basement window and we didn't even know it was there."

Ruefully Nancy admitted that this was true. She suggested that the regular doors to the cellar be securely bolted, the secret entrance to the tunnel nailed shut, and the trap door in the attic covered with a heavy trunk.

"And I'll disconnect the mechanism in the wall," she said. Taking a flashlight and a screw driver she went to the third floor and deftly removed the spring and lever.

Returning to the others, she remarked, "If we hear footsteps in this house tonight, Sheila, I'll almost agree with you that our visitor is supernatural."

Everyone went to bed early and soon fell asleep. Nancy, with the various mysteries on her mind, woke up about midnight. Wondering why, she listened intently. There was not a sound in the old house. Smiling to herself, the girl detective turned over and fell asleep once more.

Some time later she woke again. There was no mistaking the reason this time. Outside her window she heard screeching sounds. They were the same as those she had heard coming from inside the walls of Cumberland Manor! Jumping from her cot, Nancy looked out the window. She could see nothing on the lawn below.

By now the screeching had awakened Bess and George. "How horrible!" Bess cried out. "Where is it?"

She and George hopped out of bed and hurried to Nancy's side. Still nothing could be seen outside.

"I'm going down and find out what's going on!" Nancy told the cousins.

As she pulled on bathrobe and slippers, George said she and Bess would go along. Nancy grabbed up her flashlight and hurried to the first floor. She swung open the front door and rushed down the steps, beaming her light ahead of her.

In its glare stood a magnificent peacock, its fan fully spread!

"Oh!" Bess exclaimed. "The story's true!"

At that moment Sheila and Annette appeared on the porch. When the actress saw the bird, she cried out in terror, then fainted. As Sheila slumped to the floor, Bess and Annette caught her and carried the unconscious woman indoors.

"Don't worry, girls," said Annette. "Mother often does this." So George remained with Nancy.

The girl detective, meanwhile, had swung her flashlight in a wide arc over the area beyond the peacock. For a fraction of a second Nancy thought she glimpsed the figure of a crouching man, but when she turned the light back, he was gone.

By this time the peacock had recovered from the state of hypnotism produced by the light shining directly in his eyes. Folding his tail, he began to run across the lawn.

"Let's follow him, George!" Nancy whispered, keeping her flashlight trained on him.

The bird ran faster than the girls had any idea he could. They had a hard time keeping up with the peacock as they followed him across a field.

"He's going into that woods!" George said suddenly. "We may lose track of him!"

The girls ran even faster, their robes flapping in the slight breeze which had sprung up. The peacock followed a path among the trees which ended at Eddy Run. Now the bird turned left along the shore. Sloshing through the mud, Nancy and George kept pace with him.

"I wonder how far he's going?" George asked. She gave a low chuckle and added, "I've been on some crazy chases with you, Nancy Drew, but this one's the prize!"

Nancy agreed that it did seem absurd to be chasing a peacock at this hour. "If my hunch that he's going to Cumberland Manor is wrong," she said, laughing, "I'll carry you back home. But we're not far from Mr. Honsho's estate now and maybe—"

As she spoke, the peacock disappeared. Apparently he had run behind a high mass of bushes. Nancy started around the corner of the tangled shrubbery, with George close behind. Holding the flashlight directly in front of her, Nancy hoped to catch sight of the big bird again.

Instead, the light picked up a white-sheeted figure!

"The ghost!" George exclaimed.

If the masquerader had hoped to frighten the two girls into fleeing, he failed. Instead, they ran directly toward the figure which took to its heels around the shrubbery and vanished.

Nancy and George continued the search, but their advance was suddenly halted a few minutes later. A stream of water hit both girls in the face full force. It knocked them to the ground and Nancy's flashlight went out!

CHAPTER XIX

The Lone Canoeist

THE stream of water which had knocked Nancy and George to the ground and was continuing to douse them was so powerful that it left them breathless. For a moment they found it impossible to get up.

Then, as suddenly as the stream had appeared, it stopped. Thoroughly drenched and bruised, Nancy and George got to their feet. The moon was bright, lending enough light for them to see the ground clearly. In a few minutes Nancy located her flashlight and turned it on. Both the bird and the white-sheeted figure were gone.

"I wonder if the ghost took the peacock with him," George said.

Nancy did not comment. Instead, she walked on, playing the beam of her flashlight ahead and to right and left. Suddenly it shone on a brick wall.

"Cumberland Manor's just ahead," she remarked. "There must be a gate in this side of the wall. We should have investigated this spot the first time we tried to see Mr. Honsho. Apparently the ghost and the peacock are now inside."

"And what about the water? Where did that come from?" George asked.

Nancy said she was sure the stream was from a hose inside the grounds. "Since the force was so strong, I imagine someone used a fire hose."

The girls followed the trail of water which led directly to a gate. It was similar to the one which Luke Seeny had entered on the other side of the estate a few days earlier. George was inclined to think it was Luke himself who had played ghost and turned the water on the girls.

"I have a hunch Luke's trying to get even with Annette because she won't date him. He brought the peacock to Ivy Hall and let it loose to frighten her and the rest of us. Nancy, you did say you thought you saw a man in the woods."

George went on to say she thought Luke had not expected anyone to follow him and the peacock. When the two girls ran after them, Luke had taken another means of trying to frighten them. When even the ghost business did not work, he had become desperate and turned the hose on them.

"Your idea certainly sounds logical, George,"

said Nancy. "To carry on your reasoning, Luke Seeny might be the one who strapped the peacock's feet onto his shoes and also played ghost in the house."

"Exactly," said George. "And I think he knows more about Ivy Hall than we do."

Nancy said she agreed with everything George had said, except the part about Luke's wanting to get even with Annette. She still was convinced that the masquerader was after a valuable object in Ivy Hall.

"But let's find out more about Luke if we can," Nancy suggested. "Tomorrow I'll get in touch with the hotel."

As Nancy had expected, they found the gate to Cumberland Manor securely locked. Feeling sure that no one would admit them, even if they pounded on the gate, she suggested that they return to Ivy Hall.

By this time the brilliance of the moonlight made traveling so easy that Nancy turned off her flashlight. She and George made their way along the bank of Eddy Run, shivering a little from the chill night air. Suddenly Nancy grabbed George by the arm and pulled her behind a clump of bushes.

"What's up?" George asked in amazement.

Nancy whispered that she had just seen a lone figure in a canoe. "If we're wrong about Luke Seeny, that man may be the ghost," she said.

Nancy had hardly finished saying this when the occupant of the canoe flicked on a lighter and held it to a cigarette. For a brief instant his face was visible.

"Alonzo Rugby!" George said in a tense whisper.

Nancy was perplexed. If Rugby had been playing ghost, he had certainly made excellent time getting from the gate of Cumberland Manor into a canoe on Eddy Run. She mentioned this to George and added, "Maybe Alonzo and Luke are in cahoots!"

As the girls watched, Rugby picked up his paddle and began digging into the water with swift strokes. In a few minutes he was out of sight.

"Where do you figure he's going?" George asked Nancy. "And where did he come from?"

Nancy confessed to being puzzled about Rugby. He lived on a farm some distance from Eddy Run. Why was he here in a canoe at two o'clock in the morning?

"He may be coming from Bradshaw's studio," she said. "It may just be a coincidence that we've seen him tonight—he might not have anything to do with Cumberland Manor or Luke Seeny."

"Well, I'm too sleepy to figure it out," said George with a yawn.

She and Nancy started off again and twenty minutes later reached Ivy Hall. There they found Bess and the Pattersons frantic. Sheila, her daughter said, had soon come out of her faint but was nearly beside herself with worry about Nancy and George.

"Thank goodness you're here, all in one piece," the actress said. "In five minutes I was going to call the police. And now, tell me what happened. Goodness, you must have been swimming," she added, noticing the girls' wet clothes.

She insisted that before they told their story, Nancy and George change into dry pajamas, while she made hot drinks for everyone.

Ten minutes later the group gathered in Sheila's bedroom, where Bess and the Pattersons listened wide-eyed to an account of the two girls' adventure.

When the story was finished, Nancy and her chums fully expected Sheila to say that the experiment of staying at Ivy Hall had not worked and that they were all moving out. To Nancy's intense relief, however, the woman did not propose this. Instead, she said:

"Annette, if Luke Seeny is that kind of person, I'm delighted that you never dated him. Of course, he's not your type, anyway."

Her daughter agreed, glad that Sheila had momentarily forgotten the peacock. Annette said she would telephone the hotel in the morning and find out if Luke really did live there and if the clerk knew whether he had been in the night before.

At nine o'clock the following day she put in the call and learned that the young man did have a room there. He had already had breakfast and gone out.

"Would you mind telling me," Annette said in an exaggerated, coaxing drawl, "whether Mr. Seeny was in the hotel last night?"

The young man who had answered the telephone laughed. "I'm sorry, miss," he said, "but we don't keep track of our guests' comings and goings. I couldn't tell you where Mr. Seeny was last night."

After Annette had hung up, she made her report to the others, saying, "I guess I'm not much good as a detective."

Nancy smiled. "For a beginner, I'd say you did a grand job," she assured the girl. "You verified the suspect's residence, and you learned that if you want more detailed information about his habits, you'll have to start early in the morning to trail your man!"

"No, thank you," said Annette quickly. "You can carry on from here, Nancy."

"Is that our next assignment?" Bess spoke up.

Nancy shook her head. "I'm more inclined to suspect Alonzo Rugby than anybody else of being the ghost, as you know. This morning I want to drive to the farmhouse where he lives and find out something about him."

"Please don't be gone long," Sheila begged

her. "It's so much pleasanter here with you girls around."

"You're sweet to say that, Sheila. We'll be back by lunchtime," Nancy promised.

She drove off with Bess and George, and headed directly for Uplands Road. Reaching it, she slowed down to look at the name on each mailbox. Presently she reached one marked *Paget* and turned into the lane leading to the rambling farmhouse.

When the car stopped near the kitchen door, a slender, gray-haired woman, stooped and care-worn, came outside to greet them. Nancy asked the widow if Mr. Rugby were at home.

"No, Mr. Rugby's not here and he hasn't been here for a week," Mrs. Paget answered.

"Do you mean he's moved out?" Nancy asked in surprise.

"Well, I wouldn't say that. He stops in here once in a while for mail, but he never eats or sleeps here any more."

"Have you any idea where Mr. Rugby is staying?" Nancy prodded, hoping to pick up some clue to where the man spent his time when he was not at the studio.

"Well, I suppose he's stayin' with that Mr. Bradshaw he works for." Suddenly a quizzical look came into the woman's eyes. "Or isn't he?" she asked. "What you got on your mind, miss?"

CHAPTER XX

A Worrisome Gift

"I DON'T know whether Mr. Rugby is staying at the Bradshaws' or not," Nancy told Mrs. Paget. "I'm from River Heights where his sister lives. In fact, she's a neighbor of mine."

A searching look came into the widow's eyes. "How do you all like her?" she asked.

"Well, to tell you the truth," Nancy answered, "Mrs. Dondo hasn't been very friendly toward me and my family."

The young sleuth went on to say that she had heard Mrs. Dondo's brother lived in Charlottesville and frankly was curious to meet him.

"He's not like his sister," said Mrs. Paget. "Mrs. Dondo sure is a tartar. She lived here in Charlottesville, you know—and my, what a busybody she was! Things got so bad she came near bein' sued."

"Oh, really?" Bess spoke up. "What did she do?"

Mrs. Paget said that Rugby's sister began making trouble first by spreading idle gossip. "Then the woman got to accusin' people of things they never did."

"Like what?" Nancy asked quickly.

Mrs. Paget said she did not know all the details, since she lived so far out of town. It was only after Alonzo Rugby had come to board with her that friends of hers in town had warned the farm woman to be wary of the man's honesty. "But I guess he's all right," Mrs. Paget concluded.

"So you don't know any of the details as to why Mrs. Dondo moved away?" George prodded her.

"Only one thing, and that's probably not worth mentionin'," Mrs. Paget replied. "It seems that Mrs. Dondo was expectin' a letter with some money in it. When it didn't arrive, she spoke to the postman. He said it might have got mixed in with other people's mail. So Mrs. Dondo up and goes around askin' everybody. And she even had the nerve to accuse a woman she didn't like of keepin' the money. That's when Mrs. Dondo came near being sued."

Nancy and her friends were amazed. Apparently Mrs. Dondo tried to work the same racket in River Heights.

"I understand," said Nancy nonchalantly, "that Mr. Rugby has a lot of money and is very generous in helping his sister."

Mrs. Paget began to laugh. "Money! Neither one of them has got any money to speak of, but they'd sure like to have it. And what's more, they both go around puttin' on airs as if they had big bank accounts."

The girls smiled. They were getting much more information from the widow than they had hoped for! From this point on, they did not have to ask any questions. Mrs. Paget warmed to her subject.

"Those Rugbys sure are a funny family," she continued. "They seem real nice, all except for Mrs. Dondo, but they fight like cats and dogs among themselves. Left alone, Alonzo's not so bad. The only thing I got against him is his braggin'. He thinks he's a great artist."

Mrs. Paget stopped speaking long enough to take a deep breath. Then she went on, "You know folks around here were mighty sorry for Mr. Dondo. He's a nice man, and he sure had to take a lot of naggin' and fault-findin' from his wife. To tell you the truth, nobody could figure out why he put up with it."

Nancy realized that the woman still had not answered her question about Alonzo sending money to his sister. She mentioned that the Dondos lived in an attractive house, so she assumed that the husband must have a good position. If so, it seemed strange that Mrs. Dondo should be accepting money from her brother.

Mrs. Paget was scornful. "What makes you think Alonzo sends his sister any money? If you ask me, he never gave her a nickel in his life!" Suddenly Mrs. Paget sniffed. "Oh, my goodness!" she cried worriedly. "My dinner must be burned to a crisp!"

With that, she dashed toward the house. Nancy called after her, "I'm afraid we must leave now, Mrs. Paget, but we enjoyed meeting you."

"Thank you—call again!" the woman yelled back from inside the kitchen.

As the girls drove off, Nancy remarked that she could hardly wait to get to a telephone and relay the recent conversation to her father. She suggested that they stop at Susan's home, which they would pass.

"I'd like to say hello, anyway."

The three friends were disappointed not to find either Susan or Cliff at home. But Beulah was there and warmly welcomed them back. On hearing that the girls were not staying, she threw up her hands and exclaimed:

"Those ol' charms o' mine have kept the spirits from you all so far, but there's no tellin' how long their good work will last. Why don't you all stay here now that you're back safe?"

Nancy smiled. "That's very sweet of you, Beulah, but I haven't finished my work yet. You can see, though, I've kept my promise to be careful. We'll be home again in no time."

Beulah sighed and shook her head disappointedly. As Nancy went to make her phone call to Mr. Drew, Bess followed the colored woman to the kitchen. "Beulah," she said as she took a seat, "the worst thing about our mystery solving at Ivy Hall is not being able to enjoy your delicious cooking. No one can match your recipes!"

The maid grinned broadly. "That's right nice of you to say so, honey," she replied. A frown creased her forehead as she asked, "Aren't you gettin' enough to eat, Miss Bess?"

"Oh, yes," Bess said hastily. "I was just remembering your light-as-air biscuits—and chocolate cake—and fried chicken!"

Beulah burst into laughter. "I can spot a hint from a hungry girl a mile away," she said. Going into the pantry, she cut Bess a large slice from a freshly baked coconut cake.

"You're a jewel!" Bess exclaimed happily. "Thank you, Beulah!" She started eating with gusto.

As Bess finished the last bite, a car stopped in the driveway. Susan stepped from it, waved good-by to the friend who had brought her, and came inside the kitchen.

"Bess!" she cried in delight, and greeted Beulah. "I'm so glad to see you! But where are Nancy and George?"

Bess told her, then Susan said, "I was just thinking of you girls and the Pattersons." She turned to the cook. "Beulah, I'd like to have the girls take a hamper of food with them when they return to Ivy Hall. With all the excitement over there, it would be a help if Sheila and Annette didn't have to cook dinners for a couple of days."

"A good idea, Miss Susan!" Beulah said enthusiastically.

"What do we have on hand?"

The cook reported that she had made a large pot of old-fashioned vegetable soup that morning and also baked two hams. "And there's loads of fresh corn bread. And just look here—" Beulah lifted a sheet of waxed paper which covered two lemon meringue pies.

Susan complimented the maid on her efforts and asked Beulah to divide the food.

"Susan, you're so kind," Bess said appreciatively.

Beulah told them she would carry the food to the car, and started to pack it.

"And now, tell me all that has happened since you left here," Susan said to Bess, linking arms and leading her to the parlor.

Nancy and George joined them and the four sat down. Susan listened intently as the others related their story. At the end Susan remarked:

"It all seems unbelievable. And *please* be careful. It seems to me that the mystery is becoming more dangerous each day."

"And nearer a solution," Nancy declared. She rose. "I must get back to my sleuthing."

As the girls were ready to drive off, Susan said, "Don't forget that tomorrow belongs to me. We're going on a tour of gardens, you remember. Pick me up early."

Nancy said she would and waved good-by. At Ivy Hall the girls found Sheila and Annette in a flutter of excitement. A messenger boy had just been there to deliver a long, narrow box, attractively wrapped, with Annette's name on it.

Excitedly the girl raised the lid. Directly underneath lay a note which she instantly read. Her face clouded.

"It's from Luke," Annette said. "He's pleading that I make a date with him. I suppose he thinks this gift will soften me."

George chuckled. "It might at that," she said. "Let's see what he sent."

Annette unwrapped several layers of tissue paper before uncovering the gift.

"Oh!" she gasped, holding it up.

Sheila gave a shriek. "A peacock fan!" she cried out.

Covering her eyes with her hands, the actress said agitatedly, "Oh, more bad luck!"

Though Bess looked worried, Nancy and George did not take Sheila's outburst seriously. They had asked Annette to spread the fan open and now began to examine it.

"This is exquisite," Nancy remarked.

Annette was torn in her feelings. The girl was impressed with the gift, she admitted to the others, yet she could not bring herself to make a date with the sender of the fan.

"He's still a suspect in this ghost business," George observed.

Nancy suddenly snapped her fingers. "Annette," she said, "I want you to make a date with Luke Seeny."

Annette stared in astonishment. "You mean you've changed your opinion about him?" she asked.

"Not at all," Nancy replied. "But I think if you invite Luke here, we may be able to solve the mystery."

Sheila looked disapproving. "I don't want my daughter associating with such a person," she said firmly. "What's more, I insist that Annette send this fan back to him."

"Just a moment, Mother," Annette spoke up. "Let's first hear what Nancy's plan is."

"All right," Sheila conceded. "What is it you want Annette to do, Nancy?"

"Invite Luke here to dinner tomorrow evening," the young sleuth replied. "I think we can trap him into telling the truth!"

CHAPTER XXI

Mammy Johnson's Story

AFTER some deliberation Sheila Patterson finally gave her consent to Nancy's plan. She was still worried, however, that Luke Seeny might become even more of a nuisance than he had been before.

"Don't be concerned," said George. "If anyone can set a trap for that cowboy, Nancy can!"

"That's right," Bess agreed, and then announced that the girls had a very different kind of surprise for the Pattersons. She went out to the car and began bringing in the parcels of food.

On seeing them, Sheila began to cry. "Oh, people around here have been so kind," she said. "It makes me feel bad that I'm not in a position to return their favors."

"I'm sure you can," said Bess kindly. "Everyone here would surely love to see you act. I'm certain there'll be an opportunity for you to put on a performance for them."

Sheila admitted she already had been asked by Susan Carr to put on a skit for a charity performance in a few weeks. "I really haven't felt up to it and have delayed replying," the actress said. "But now you give me a new incentive, Bess. I'll do it!"

"And I'd like to entertain here," said Annette wistfully, "if the grounds were only fixed up."

After Sheila and the girls had eaten part of the sumptuous food from the Carrs' larder, George proposed that the group go outside and tidy up the grounds. The Pattersons were delighted and the rest of the day was spent working with lawn mowers, rakes, spades, and shovels. By suppertime the grass, flower beds, and shrubbery looked trim and well-kept.

Sheila smiled in delight. "Isn't it beautiful?" she said. "Oh, I just love this place really." Then she frowned. "If only the mystery of Ivy Hall could be cleared up!"

"I have a hunch," said Nancy, "that it won't be long before the ghost is caught."

The actress flashed her a hopeful smile. She did not know that all the time Nancy had been working in the garden, she had been keeping her eyes open for clues and also planning a strategic campaign to learn the truth from Luke Seeny. Nancy now suggested that Annette call him at his hotel.

Annette went inside to phone. She returned

a few minutes later, saying that Luke would be there the following evening.

The night passed without incident. Sheila was in good spirits the next morning and did not mind when Nancy set off early with Bess and George to pick up Susan for the Garden Tour. "I know you'll love it," she said.

The weather was perfect. As they viewed the various show gardens, the visitors gasped in wonder and admiration. Bess declared she had never seen such magnificent flowering shrubs. George was particularly entranced by the many varieties of iris, which was her favorite flower.

"I can't decide what I like best," Nancy remarked. "But the sweet-smelling magnolias are heavenly."

At each home Nancy would first make a tour of the garden, then stop to ask the host or hostess and the servants if they had ever heard of a family named Greystone in the area. Failing, she would inquire about a stained-glass window, which portrayed a knight with a peacock on his shield. To her disappointment, no one had seen such a window.

Toward the end of the afternoon Susan directed her friends to one of the oldest estates in the vicinity. The present owner, named Van Buskirk, had bought the place intact, and all the servants had remained.

"There's one old mammy here you'll love,"

Susan told the girls. "She's quite infirm and spends most of her time in a rocking chair. But she has a fabulous memory and is full of good stories of the old South. Nancy, if Mammy Johnson is feeling well enough to talk, she may be able to give you some helpful information."

Nancy was thrilled. After she and her friends had admired the creamy-pink flowering magnolias, the lavender-tinted plum blossoms, and the extensive boxwood-enclosed beds of azaleas and tulips, they went to the old slave quarters. The Van Buskirks had modernized them as accommodations for their servants.

Susan knocked on the kitchen door. It was opened by a slight, somewhat stooped, white-haired colored woman.

"Howdy, Mis' Carr," she said in a low, soft voice.

"Hello, Mammy Johnson. I've brought some friends of mine from the North," Susan said. "They'd like to come in and ask you some questions if they may."

"Please to come in, young ladies," said the elderly woman, smiling. She held the door open while they entered and found chairs. Susan took care to direct the others away from the colored woman's favorite rocker. She motioned for Mammy Johnson to sit down and then introduced the girls one by one.

"Miss Drew is a girl detective," Susan explained.

"And she's trying to find some trace of a family who may have once lived around here. Their name was Greystone."

Mammy Johnson put one hand to her fore-head as if thinking hard. Finally she said, "I never rightly heard of a family named Greystone, but I did know 'bout one named Grayce. My mammy's grandma worked for 'em." She smiled. "Do you s'pose, Miss Drew, that they all might have changed their name when they came to America?"

Nancy was excited to hear this. "You say when they came to America? Where did the Grayces come from?"

"It was England," Mammy Johnson answered. "I say maybe they changed their name, 'cause my mammy told me that once, when Mis' Grayce was awful sick—she come near dyin'—well, she cried out, delirious-like, 'Please forgive us, Lord Grey-stone. We done wrong to come here. Please forgive us!' "

Startled, the callers stared at one another. Nancy had risen quickly from her chair and went to stand alongside Mammy Johnson. Mean-while, Nancy had been figuring out in what year the woman's great-grandmother might have lived. She decided it could well have been a few years after 1850!

"Where is the Grayce family now?" Nancy asked excitedly.

"Oh, they all done died off long ago," Mammy Johnson said, looking out the window sadly.

There was a moment of sympathetic silence among the listeners. Then Nancy asked, "Mammy Johnson, did your mother ever tell you that the Grayce family had a stained-glass window in their home?"

The old woman shook her head. "But if there was one, maybe it's still there. Why don't you go look for it?"

"Where is the house?" Nancy asked, her heart thumping wildly as she waited for the answer.

Mammy Johnson said the place was only a few miles away. "The name of it is—let me think— oh, yes, I remember now. It's called Ivy Hall."

"Hypers!" George cried out.

The old woman looked at the girl, not understanding her outburst. George quickly explained that the girls were staying at Ivy Hall.

"We did look for a stained-glass window there, but haven't found any," Bess put in. "It was probably taken out."

Susan arose and said they must leave. She and Nancy thanked Mammy Johnson for telling them what she knew, then said good-by.

As the group headed for Susan's home, the conversation was full of speculation. Were the Grayce and Greystone families one and the same? If so, was Ivy Hall, the former Grayce home, the original property of the Greystones from England?

Had the stained-glass window once been there?
And was it hidden there now?

Finally George chuckled. "I suppose, Nancy,
that now you'll want to tear the place down brick
by brick to find out."

Her friend smiled. "Maybe Luke Seeny will
save us the trouble." Nancy looked at her watch.
"He'll get there to dinner before we do if we
don't hurry."

After they had dropped Susan at Seven Oaks,
the girls reviewed their campaign for the evening. Each one was to play a part in trying to
trick Luke into revealing whether or not he had
been the ghost.

Annette's guest, immaculately dressed, arrived
at seven o'clock. He seemed very poised and polite. Luke was greeted in very friendly fashion
and seemed pleased to meet the girls from River
Heights.

"I'm sure that he's not suspicious of us,"
Nancy thought.

Conversation remained light until dessert was
served. Then Bess asked the visitor seriously if
he knew Alonzo Rugby.

"No, I never heard of him," Luke replied.

Nancy, watching the cowboy closely, was convinced he was telling the truth. Presently
George brought up the subject of Garden Week
and remarked that everyone in the locale was disappointed that Mr. Honsho would not open his

estate to the public. "Why won't he?" she asked.

Luke frowned. "I don't know. He's kind of a recluse—doesn't have much to do with people who live around these parts. When he heard I was visiting here from Oklahoma, he sent for me. Said he wanted to find out all about my home state."

"Oh, you don't work for him?" Nancy asked casually. "We noticed that you had a key to the estate."

The young man reddened. "Mr. Honsho never leaves the grounds," he replied. "He gave me a key."

Bess gave a great sigh. "It must be beautiful behind those brick walls," she said dramatically. "Tell us about it, Luke."

"Not much to tell," he replied, unimpressed. "There are nice flowers, trees, and bushes. That's about all."

Nancy mentioned the strange sounds the girls had heard coming from Cumberland Manor. Looking straight at Luke, she asked, "Does Mr. Honsho keep peacocks?"

For the first time, Luke winced. He did not answer the question at once. When he did speak again, he merely said, "I'm not privileged to discuss Mr. Honsho's private business."

But Nancy was inwardly exulting. Luke's reaction to the mention of peacocks must have some bearing on the mystery!

When the meal was over, Annette asked Luke if he would like to see the house and some of its secrets. The young man's eyes popped wide open as he answered, "Indeed I would!"

Annette's eyes, in contrast, were twinkling. Turning to the three girls, she said, "You and Mother must come too. I think you'd enjoy seeing some of the things."

This was all part of the prearranged plan to trap Luke, but Nancy, Bess, and George were thunderstruck when Annette led them to the old library and removed a section of the built-in bookcase. Behind it was a wall safe, its combination lock gone. There was nothing in the safe itself.

"I guess the former owners took everything out of here," Annette remarked.

Luke showed great surprise and interest in the hiding place. Was he faking?

Annette now led the group into the kitchen, where she tugged at one of the hearthstones and lifted it. To the amazement of the visiting girls, and apparently Luke, a very narrow stairway was revealed, leading downward.

"I think it was a storage room," said Sheila. "There's nothing down there now but a lot of empty bottles."

Annette said that during the day, when the three girls had been away, she and her mother had instituted a search of Ivy Hall.

"The next place I want to show you, Luke," said Annette, "is our attic."

All eyes watched the guest closely. They were sure that this time he gave an involuntary start.

When the group reached the third floor, Bess pointed out the picture of the cavalier. Then George adroitly steered Luke toward the trunk from which the girls were sure the ghost had removed a sheet.

"Luke Seeny, this is the hide-out of Ivy Hall's ghost," George intoned in a sepulchral voice.

The girls laughed and Annette said, "Our tour is almost over, Luke, so don't worry."

Going over to him she locked an arm into his and deliberately guided him toward the trap door from which the trunk had been removed. Pausing directly on top of the door, she pointed out an antique water jug.

"Isn't it quaint?" she asked.

In the meantime, Nancy had moved to the side wall and was now pushing back the secret panel. "Luke," she said, "there's a lever back here that—"

A look of terror came over the young man's face.

"Don't touch it!" he almost screamed at her. "Don't you dare touch it!"

Luke jumped off the trap door, dragging Annette with him!

CHAPTER XXII

A Ghost Confesses

FOR several seconds there was unbroken silence in the attic. Sheila and the girls waited for Luke Seeny to say something after his sudden outburst. When he kept perfectly still, just staring ahead of him, Nancy finally said:

"So you're the ghost of Ivy Hall!"

"I'm not," Luke denied, but there was no conviction in his voice.

As he lapsed into silence again, George brought up the subject of Mr. Honsho. "You work for him and brought a peacock from his place over here the other night, didn't you?"

"I told you before I can't tell you anything about Mr. Honsho," Luke cried out defiantly. "Say, what is this, the third degree?"

The others looked toward Nancy to carry on the conversation. To their astonishment, she did not use a stern tone as she began to speak to Luke. Instead, she smiled at him and said in a coaxing manner:

"It's just no use, Luke. There is too much evidence against you—your knowledge of the mechanism that opens the trap door, your leaving the trunk open after you took the sheet out of it, the bronze peacock's foot strapped to your own shoe and lost in the mud—"

"Don't say any more!" Luke begged. "I don't know how you found out all these things. You're a pretty smart girl, but I haven't done anything wrong—really I haven't."

"Suppose you tell us the whole story," Nancy suggested. "We'll go downstairs and sit in some comfortable chairs."

"And you won't call the police?" the young man asked fearfully.

Sheila Patterson spoke up. "We'll answer that question after we hear your story."

Nancy was afraid the actress might say more and spoil everything. But the woman did not speak as they descended to the first floor.

By the time they were seated in the old parlor of Ivy Hall, Luke seemed completely crestfallen. He was very pale, and as he began to speak, his voice quivered.

"I worked as a cowboy in Oklahoma. My parents had no money and the only cash I ever had was what I earned. I saved a little and decided to try my luck here.

"What I told you about Mr. Honsho getting in touch with me," Luke continued, "was pretty near the truth. Right after I got here, the hotel manager asked me if I'd like a job. When I said yes, he told me that Mr. Honsho was looking for somebody to help around his place. I rented a bicycle and rode there."

The Oklahoman went on to say that while working at Cumberland Manor he had found an old diary which belonged to a former owner of the estate. In it he had found a notation which mentioned that there was a very unusual stained-glass window on the neighboring property.

"That same day I happened to see an article in a copy of *Continental* magazine which told about Sir Richard Greystone's offer to the finder of a certain stained-glass window. I thought the window might be hidden at Ivy Hall and I decided to find out."

Luke hung his head. "First I tried to date Annette, so that I could get a good look at the inside of the house. When she refused, I figured the only way to find out about the window was to get inside the place somehow. I decided to try scaring the Pattersons away by bringing over one of Mr. Honsho's peacocks—he has a flock of them. I'd heard stage folks are superstitious about peacocks."

Annette looked at the young man in disgust. "You nearly succeeded in driving us out," she said. "If it hadn't been for Nancy Drew, we probably wouldn't be here tonight."

"Please go on with your story, Luke," Nancy requested.

The cowboy said that after he had failed to scare the Pattersons away, he had risked making entries into the old house at night. He had become pretty well acquainted with it, even to finding the mechanism which worked the trap door.

"So it was your footsteps we heard!" Annette remarked.

Luke nodded. When the girls had nearly discovered him in the attic, he had hidden behind the secret panel. He had seized the opportunity to open the trap door and send Nancy and George down the slide, convinced that this would frighten the group away from Ivy Hall.

Luke said he had used the slide himself previously and had found the secret opening into the kitchen. He had figured that the two girls would also locate it and escape.

Bess interrupted Luke to ask, "Why did you nearly scare me out of my wits playing ghost in the attic? You could have stayed behind the panel until I left."

"I suppose I could have," Luke replied. "But you just seemed like the scary type and I thought my trick would sure drive you all away."

"And you played the same trick," George spoke

up, "when Nancy and I chased you and the peacock over to Cumberland Manor."

Luke admitted that he had taken the sheet along and hidden it in some bushes. When his attempt to scare Nancy and George had failed, he had turned Mr. Honsho's fire hose on them.

"I guess I'm just a good-for-nothing," the cowboy said. "But I don't want to go to jail. Please don't call the police," he begged again.

Nancy said this decision lay with the Pattersons. "What I'd like to know is, did you find any clue to the missing peacock window?"

"No, I didn't," Luke said. "You've got to believe me."

He looked pleadingly at Sheila Patterson, who blinked several times. Then she said, "I suppose we all make mistakes, especially if we're trying too hard to make quick money."

Luke looked relieved. "I'll tell you what," he burst out. "To show you I'm on the level, I'll take you all over to Cumberland Manor and introduce you to Mr. Honsho. Then you can ask him to open his place for Garden Week."

The unexpected offer surprised the group so much that they did not immediately answer Luke. The thought flitted through Nancy's mind that if he was not sincere, he might be making this offer so that he could escape. He probably would suggest that the group meet Mr. Honsho the next day, and in the meantime he himself would disappear.

"When do you want us to go?" she asked the young man.

"Why, right away," he answered. "Mr. Honsho doesn't go to bed until very late."

Nancy relaxed. It began to look as if Luke Seeny were not a malicious character—but a weak person who could not resist temptation.

"We'll go with you," Nancy said, without promising whether or not the police would be notified later of Luke's misdemeanor.

Nancy asked Sheila and Annette if they wanted to go along. Both said they would be delighted to meet Mr. Honsho. Nancy went for the car and the whole group piled in.

When they reached Cumberland Manor she parked, and the group walked down the path by the beam of Nancy's flashlight. After Luke had unlocked the gate, the visitors stepped inside and the young man carefully locked it again.

"Follow me," he said, and led the way among towering trees and lovely gardens to the old stone mansion. It was English Tudor in style, and the lights within seemed to beckon the visitors hospitably.

Luke suddenly gave a peculiar whistle to announce their approach. After he had repeated it a second time, the front door of the mansion opened. A slender man of medium build, with dark skin and hair, came outside.

"Mr. Honsho," Luke called out, "I've brought you some visitors."

Although the callers realized that the Indian gentleman must be very much surprised and perhaps annoyed, he gave no evidence of it. Cordially he invited them into the house, which was furnished exquisitely. Luke introduced the visitors one by one and told where they were from, adding that the Pattersons had recently bought Ivy Hall.

"I am pleased to meet you all," said their host. He spoke flawless English with a British accent. Then he turned to Luke and with a smile said, "I presume the visitors have learned our little secret?"

"Yes, they have, sir," Luke replied. "Miss Drew is an amateur detective. She recognized the screeching of the peacocks."

Mr. Honsho looked at the girl in combined perplexity and admiration. He made no comment on the subject, however. Instead, he said, "Is it because of my peacocks that I have the honor of your visit this evening?"

"Not entirely," said Nancy. "I'm a cousin of Mrs. Clifford Carr, one of your neighbors. She's on the Garden Week committee. Because of the fact that I love to solve mysteries, she asked me if I would try to find out why you refused to open your gardens to the public."

Mr. Honsho chuckled. "And you know the answer? That I would not do it because I heard some people in this area are superstitious about peacocks?"

Nancy smiled. "Whatever I thought, I did not mention it to anyone. But I assure you, Mr. Honsho, you have perhaps been misinformed about Americans believing that peacocks bring bad luck. Most of us, the same as people in your country, think that the birds are very beautiful and we admire them."

The Indian's face broke into a broad smile. "I am relieved to hear that," he said, "because I am very proud of my beautiful birds. Come, I will show them to you."

After turning on several switches which lighted up the grounds, he led the way back of the house to an extensive wire enclosure. In it, roosting among the trees, were a large number of birds. Mr. Honsho gave a low cooing sound and instantly one of them left its roost and flew down to him. It was pure white and very stately looking.

"This bird is sacred to us Indians," Mr. Honsho said, gazing affectionately at the beautiful feathered creature. "If you can assure me, Miss Drew, that visitors to my place will not injure my peacocks, I will be happy to open my gates."

The visitors exclaimed their thanks and voiced their admiration of his proud-looking birds. "I hope every one of them will spread its fan when the visitors come," said Bess.

Mr. Honsho bade his callers good night, adding that he would leave the lights on until Luke had escorted the group outside the gate.

"Isn't Mr. Honsho charming?" Bess burst out as they drove off. "And so different from what I expected."

"He's been very good to me," said Luke. On the way back to Ivy Hall, the cowboy was silent until they reached the house. Then he asked apprehensively, "Have I exonerated myself?"

Sheila looked at him steadfastly. Then she said, "Luke, I think maybe you've learned your lesson. I shan't prosecute you."

Meanwhile, Annette had gone into the house and now came outside with the feather fan. "I want you to take this with you," she said, handing it to Luke.

A look of pain crossed his face. "I made it for you myself," he said. "Please keep the fan. It'll help to make up for all the trouble I caused."

"Well, if you insist. And thank you," the girl answered.

Luke expressed his gratitude to everyone for their leniency toward him, hopped astride his bicycle, and pedaled off into the darkness.

"I mustn't start liking him," Annette remarked,

as she admired the fan. "But I do feel sorry for him."

Bess sighed. "Pity is akin to love, Annette. Look out!"

As the girls from River Heights were preparing for bed, George patted Nancy on the shoulder. "Congratulations, old pal. You've solved one of the mysteries of Charlottesville!"

Nancy grinned. Now she could concentrate on the others. She was the first one up the following morning and at once telephoned to Susan Carr.

"Hi, Sue!" she said. "Good news! Mr. Honsho is going to open his gardens to visitors this morning and for the rest of Garden Week!"

Susan exclaimed, "I don't know how you did it!" Nancy told her briefly what had happened.

Susan said she would notify the rest of the committee at once and each of them would make phone calls to spread the word that Cumberland Manor would be open to the public.

The group at Ivy Hall had a quick breakfast and set off immediately for Mr. Honsho's estate. He greeted them cordially and said that Luke had come directly back to Cumberland Manor after leaving the girls. He had worked all night to get the place in readiness for display.

The Indian told them that Luke had confessed everything, including taking the peacock. He felt the young man sincerely regretted his actions.

Nancy and her friends were glad to hear this.

They spent the whole day welcoming the many visitors to the Cumberland Manor gardens. Men and women especially admired the exquisite peacocks. To the delight of the crowd, many of the birds strutted around with their fans opened.

It was late in the afternoon when Nancy and her friends returned to Ivy Hall. All were weary and declared that as soon as supper was over, they were going to bed.

"I'm warning everybody now," said Nancy, "that I'm getting up at the crack of dawn to hunt for the stained-glass window."

"I'll be with you," said George, and Bess nodded her agreement.

By this time Sheila had unlocked the great front door and the group walked in.

Suddenly the actress shrieked. "Oh, my home! My home!" she cried out.

Everyone stared in stupefied amazement at what they saw. Walls, floors, and ceilings had been hacked. The place was a shambles!

CHAPTER XXIII

Rifled Luggage

THE hysterical state of Sheila Patterson became so alarming that the girls forgot everything else. The actress alternately laughed and cried, and continuously pointed to the hacked walls, floors, and ceilings of Ivy Hall.

"We must call a doctor," said Annette. She was on the verge of hysterics herself.

George hurried to the phone while the others endeavored to calm Sheila, but this proved to be impossible. There was nothing to do except wait for Dr. Tillett to arrive.

"We must notify the police also," Nancy spoke up, and phoned headquarters immediately.

Two officers arrived at the same time Dr. Tillett did. Sheila was put to bed and a short while later the physician announced that she was asleep and by morning the actress would have recovered from her shock.

In the meantime, Nancy had answered all the questions which the police had asked, then had shown them through the house. They found that entry had been made by smashing a dining-room window. The various secret places of the mansion were revealed and investigated. There was no clue to the intruder.

One of the officers, named Hanley, said, "The fellow must have worn gloves and there are no distinct footprints."

The two policemen had about concluded their work when Bess cried out from the girls' bedroom. Nancy and the officers rushed to see what the trouble was.

"That horrible burglar," Bess exclaimed, "mussed up all our clothes!" She explained that upon opening her suitcase she had found everything in it topsy-turvy. "And my beautiful new slip is gone!" Bess added woefully.

Quickly Nancy's and George's baggage was examined. Their suitcases, too, were in a state of disarray and several new articles of lingerie were missing.

Officer Hanley frowned. "That's a strange combination of burglarizing," he remarked. "Why anyone would hack up a house and then steal women's clothes doesn't make sense. But there's one answer. Two intruders—a man and a woman—may have been here."

The policemen examined the room for clues

to establish this fact. Finally Officer Hanley remarked that there were none.

"We'll report our findings to the chief," he told the girls.

After the men left, Nancy and George went to board up the window which the intruder had smashed. Then they made sure everything was locked tightly before going to their room. Bess, already in bed, asked if Nancy had any theories as to the person who had been in the house.

"Well, Luke Seeny is exonerated," Nancy replied. "Which, to my mind, pinpoints the suspect as Alonzo Rugby."

"Do you think there was any reason for rifling our suitcases, except to steal the lingerie?"

"Yes, I do, Bess. I believe Rugby was looking for letters I might have had from Lord Greystone regarding the peacock window."

"Then you don't think a woman was here too?" George spoke up.

Nancy shrugged. Then she smiled. "Maybe one of these days Alonzo Rugby's loving sister will be wearing our brand-new lingerie, girls."

"Ugh!" said Bess.

George turned out the light and soon the girls were asleep. The next morning they found Sheila feeling well and in complete control of her emotions. She said that damage to the house was covered by insurance, and she would attend to having repairs made as soon as possible.

After breakfast Nancy announced that she was going to make an even more exhaustive search of the house. "First I'm going to look for clues to the hidden window. Then I hope to learn, if possible, whether or not the burglar discovered the window and took it away."

All four girls joined in the search but two hours later they admitted defeat. They sat down in the old parlor with Sheila to discuss what to do next.

"Well, I know what I'm going to do," said George, rising. "Go upstairs and wash my hair. It's so full of dust, I can't stand it."

She left the others and climbed the steps. Halfway up she stopped short, leaned down, and picked up a small piece of oblong-shaped dark-red glass. Excitedly George hurried down the stairs and showed it to the others.

"Do you suppose the burglar dropped this?" she asked.

Nancy took the piece of glass and held it up to the light. The glass was wavy and looked very old. "Someone familiar with leaded windows did drop this," she said.

Sheila burst into tears. "Oh, that dreadful man did find our stained-glass window! Now there won't be a reward for any of us or a chance to sell the window!"

Nancy had to admit it would be pretty difficult to prove that the old window had been stolen from Ivy Hall. The finder could easily say it had been found some place else. Then, suddenly, a new thought came to her. Maybe the red glass was not part of the window for which they were searching!

"There's still hope, Sheila," she said kindly, and told what she suspected.

"You think this man Rugby dropped the piece of glass?" Annette asked.

Nancy nodded. "I'm going to find out if I possibly can where Rugby is staying and where he was yesterday."

"How are you going to do that?" Sheila questioned.

"I'll enlist my cousin Susan's aid," Nancy replied. "I'll ask Sue to call Mrs. Bradshaw and casually ask if Rugby is their house guest."

Going to the phone, she called the Carr home. When Susan answered, she told her what had happened at Ivy Hall.

"How dreadful!" Susan said. "That lovely old house! I'll find out right away what you want to know and call you, Nancy."

The return call came ten minutes later. Alonzo Rugby had not been staying with the Bradshaws and had not slept in the studio, either. Mrs. Bradshaw did not know where the man had been the day before, because she and her husband had gone on a tour of gardens, and assumed that Rugby had worked in the studio all day as usual.

"Thanks, Sue."

"Glad to help, Nancy. And let me know if I can do anything else."

Nancy returned to the parlor and said, "Rugby had a marvelous opportunity to spend hours here yesterday. I think we should do some sleuthing and see if we can find out where he's staying."

She outlined her plan. The girls would get a canoe and hide it on Eddy Run near Bradshaw's studio.

"If Alonzo leaves in a car, we'll follow him with ours. But if he goes off in a canoe, we'll trail him on the water."

Once more Susan Carr's aid was enlisted. She borrowed a canoe for Nancy, and Cliff brought it over in the station wagon. The girls carried it Indian-style down to the stream and paddled it up near Waverly. They hid the canoe among some bushes, then walked back to Ivy Hall.

"What time do you think we should start our spying?" George asked Nancy.

The young sleuth felt that there was no necessity of doing anything before five o'clock, the time that Rugby normally left the studio. Sheila prepared an early supper for the girls, then they set off in the car.

After parking near the driveway into Waverly, they walked through the woods, bordering the road, down to the studio. From among the trees they could easily look into the building. Rugby was moving about but showed no signs of leaving.

"We may have a long wait," said Nancy. "I really hope he doesn't leave until after dark."

As if acceding to her wish, Rugby stayed inside the studio. As hour after hour went by, Bess became tired of the vigil and suggested that they leave.

"I wouldn't think of it," said George firmly, and Nancy agreed.

As darkness came, the girls moved closer to the studio. The windows were open and they could hear Rugby mumbling to himself. There was only one small light in the studio. This was near the telephone.

Presently Rugby consulted his watch. Then he picked up the telephone and gave a number in New York City.

"Whom do you suppose he's calling?" Bess whispered.

The other two girls did not reply, for just then the operator made the connection and Alonzo Rugby began to speak. "Is this Sir Richard Greystone?"

The three girls gripped one another's arms as the suspect went on, "You will? That's great. I'm certainly glad you're going to fly down. The

*Apparently Rugby had found the missing
window*

old peacock window is in perfect condition, Sir Richard. Wait until you see it!"

The listeners were stunned. Apparently Alonzo Rugby had found the missing window. Had he stolen it from Ivy Hall? Would he get the reward for locating it and perhaps even sell the window to Sir Richard Greystone?

"Isn't this awful!" Bess exclaimed in a whisper.

As soon as Rugby had completed his phone call, he flicked off the light, came to the door, and walked outside. He locked the studio, lighted a cigarette, and set off for Eddy Run.

"Come on!" said Nancy.

Quiet as mice, the girls trailed him. Reaching the water, the man stepped into a canoe and paddled off. His pursuers broke into a run, launched their own craft, and climbed in. With Nancy in the prow and George in the stern they paddled after the suspect.

Rugby, familiar with the stream, zigzagged among the rocks. Nancy and George tried to follow his course but found this impossible.

Suddenly the girls' canoe rammed a stone. There was a splintering sound and within moments water gushed into the craft!

CHAPTER XXIV

Captured!

"What luck!" George exclaimed in disgust.

Further pursuit of Alonzo was impossible. Paddling at top speed, he was already out of sight. The girls paddled their rapidly filling canoe as close to land as they could, then waded ashore, pulling the craft after them.

"This thing is a wreck," said Bess. "We'd better win that reward, so we can pay for it."

Wet and discouraged, the girls plodded back to their car and returned to Ivy Hall. The Pattersons were overwhelmed by the news regarding the stained-glass window.

"I told you peacocks bring actresses bad luck!" Sheila said. "No one ever had any worse luck than I've had recently."

"Sheila," Nancy spoke up, "it's just possible Alonzo Rugby has not found Greystone's window at all."

The others stared at the girl detective in amazement and Sheila asked, "Whatever makes you think that?"

Nancy went on excitedly, "I shouldn't be surprised if Rugby is pulling a hoax of some kind. He's probably skillful at making stained glass and may know how to imitate the wavy effect of the old variety."

George interrupted. "Then the piece I found may be a sample of his work?"

"Yes. It's possible Rugby has put together a stained-glass window, planning to fool Sir Richard into buying the imitation—or, at least, getting the reward."

"Oh, Nancy," said Sheila, "you figure things out so magnificently. Can this mean the missing window may still be at Ivy Hall?"

"Yes, Sheila. And I suggest that we start early tomorrow on another search."

Next morning the group had only a small breakfast, then the feverish hunt began. The girls separated. Nancy decided to study the outside of the house. She walked round and round it many times, gazing at the architecture from every angle. Seeing nothing unusual, Nancy next began carefully tearing off sections of the ivy to look at the bricks closely. Presently she came to the wall of the old library. Here the bricks seemed to be of a slightly different shade from those in the rest of the building.

The young sleuth was curious. Could the missing window possibly have been in this section and bricked over? Calling the others, Nancy pointed out her find.

"Let's see what's on the other side," she suggested excitedly, and they all rushed into the house.

As they entered the gloomy old library, Nancy said, "This time, Sheila, with your permission, I'd like to do a little hacking. I'll try not to tear up the walls too much."

"Go ahead," the actress said. She hardly dared hope that Nancy was going to make an important discovery.

Picking up an old fire tong, Nancy swung the handle at the plaster. Pieces began to chip off and soon there was a hole large enough to reveal what was behind it.

"A brick wall!" said Sheila. Disappointment showed in her eyes.

But Nancy was not discouraged. "If there was a window here at one time," she said, "it may have been bricked up on both sides. I can soon find out by comparing it with the wall in the next room."

In the old parlor Nancy chipped away some of the plaster on the wall that adjoined the suspected one. Behind the plaster were studs and lathe, with a brick wall beyond. Feeling that she had practically proved her point about the house having an inner and an outer brick wall only in a section of the library, she requested permission of Sheila to take out a few of the bricks.

"Go ahead," the actress said excitedly. "*I must* know if you're right."

Annette found some tools. Very cautiously Nancy used a chisel and hammer between two of the bricks. Little by little the old sand cement came away and finally she was able to lift out one of the bricks. Now she shone her flashlight inside.

Revealed were parts of a red and a blue section of leaded glass!

"The window!" Sheila cried out. "Oh, how thrilling!"

Nancy's heart was thumping wildly. "We must go immediately and try to head off Rugby before he collects any money from Sir Richard."

"How can we find Rugby?" Bess asked. "I'm sure that he's not at the studio."

"I think he has a hideaway somewhere up Eddy Run," Nancy replied. "So let's get another canoe and try to locate the place."

Sheila and Annette said they would remain at Ivy Hall and guard the hidden window. With victory so close, they did not want anything to happen to it.

"Let's start!" Nancy said to Bess and George, eager to be off.

"But where are we going to find a canoe?"
George reminded her.

For answer, Nancy hurried into the house and
telephoned to Mr. Honsho. She inquired if he
had a canoe, and learning that he did, Nancy
asked if the girls might borrow it. The Indian
graciously agreed. He would have Luke take it
down to the water immediately.

By the time Nancy and her friends reached the
spot, the young man was waiting. The three
girls thanked him, climbed into the canoe, and
started off.

They paddled for nearly a mile without seeing a building which might be Rugby's hide-out.
Then, among a grove of trees, Nancy spotted a
rather tumble-down farmhouse. From the un-
kempt condition of the grounds, the place appeared to be uninhabited.

"Let's look," she urged. "This would make a
good hide-out."

The girls beached the canoe and started up a
tangled, weed-choked path to the house. Reaching it, they looked about. No one was in sight.
Nancy knocked. There was no response.

"Suppose we investigate a little," George suggested, gazing at the dwelling and a small barn
across a lane.

One side of the house was almost entirely ob-
scured by high shrubbery. Nancy, Bess, and

George squeezed through an opening in it, then gasped. In the wall confronting them was a stained-glass window which in every way fitted the description of the missing one!

"Oh—" Bess cried out.

Before she could say more, there was a rustle in the bushes behind the girls. Turning, they looked straight into the questioning eyes of Alonzo Rugby!

Instantly the girls were on the alert. Alonzo Rugby must not know that they suspected the window of being a copy. Nancy, smiling pleasantly, was the first to speak. "This is exquisite, isn't it?"

The man's suspicious expression relaxed. "Do you think so?" he countered.

George and Bess took their cue from Nancy and began to rave about the beautiful colors and the amazing lifelike quality of the knight and the peacock.

"Its real beauty shows up from inside the house," said Rugby enthusiastically. "Come in."

The three girls followed him inside the deserted house. From there the window looked lovely with the light shining through it. But Nancy strongly doubted that it was the old masterpiece.

Bess, with the same thought, suddenly blurted

out, "Mr. Rugby, is this an old window or did you make it?"

Her words seemed to act as a signal. Without warning, a heavy-set man and a woman appeared from an adjoining room. The woman was Mrs. Dondo! They carried rope and gags with them.

"So! You little spy!" Nancy's neighbor hissed at her.

"Cut the chatter," said Rugby, who had grabbed a piece of rope. "Let's tie these kids up!"

A fierce struggle followed, but the girls were no match for the two men and Mrs. Dondo who fought like a tigress. Nancy, Bess, and George were quickly overpowered and securely bound. Gags were stuffed into their mouths, then the three girls were carried outside and into the barn across the lane. One by one they were lifted up a ladder and deposited in the hayloft.

Laughing scornfully, Mrs. Dondo and the men left the barn.

CHAPTER XXV

The Secret of Ivy Hall

THE struggles of Nancy and her friends to free themselves proved hopeless. Now they squirmed through the hay, trying to get close enough together, so they could work on one another's bonds. But in their awkward positions, they could make no headway on the tight knots.

Ten minutes later, as the girls rested for a moment, they heard a car arriving. It stopped, two car doors banged, then a voice with a cheery English accent called out:

"Hello there!"

From their hayloft prison the girls pictured Rugby appearing from the house. A second later, to their dismay, they heard him say, "Hello, Lord Greystone. Glad to see you."

Then they could hear Rugby being introduced by Sir Richard to a second Englishman named

Mr. Peters. After chatting for a few minutes, the men apparently went inside the house.

"I *must* get loose and stop Rugby!" Nancy told herself determinedly.

She raised herself up and looked around for some other means of loosening the girls' bonds.

Suddenly her eyes detected a scythe in a far corner of the hayloft. Dragging herself to it, Nancy began to saw through the bindings on her wrists. When her hands were free she took the gag from her mouth, then cut through the rope which bound her ankles.

"I'll have yours off in a minute," she whispered excitedly to Bess and George. When the cousins stood up, free of the ropes and gags, she said urgently, "Come on! Hurry! We must stop Rugby!"

Just as the girls started down the ladder of the haymow, Sir Richard came from the house. In a clear-cut voice he said:

"Mr. Rugby, I can't tell you and your sister what this means to me. To think that at last I have found the window which belonged to my family centuries ago. Come with me to the hotel and I will give you the reward money immediately."

"I'll follow in my car," Rugby replied.

By this time Nancy was racing from the barn, with Bess and George at her heels. Disheveled,

and with wisps of straw in her blond hair, she
rushed up to the two visitors.

As the men looked at her in surprise, Nancy
gasped. The taller of the two looked amazingly
like the cavalier portrait in the Patterson attic.

"Sir Richard Greystone?" she addressed him.

"Why, yes," the ruddy-complexioned man replied.

In his early fifties, he was prematurely white-
haired, and had a small bristly black mustache.

Rugby looked at the girls with fury in his eyes,
but in a forced, pleasant tone of voice he said, "If
you'll excuse us, girls, we're in a hurry."

Ignoring him, Nancy went on, "Sir Richard,
I'm Nancy Drew from River Heights. You may
remember my father, Carson Drew, called you a
short time ago and said if the window had not
been found, I was going to hunt for it. I'm sorry
to intrude, but I don't think you should give Mr.
Rugby the reward money until he can prove that
the stained-glass window here is the one you've
been looking for."

At this remark Mrs. Dondo leaped toward
Nancy with the agility of a panther about to kill.
"Why, you little hussy!" she shouted furiously.
"Get out of here—this is none of your business!"

Her outburst shocked Sir Richard Greystone
and Mr. Peters. Alonzo Rugby looked confused
for a moment, then he collected his wits.

Taking hold of the Englishman's arm, he said

smoothly, "Don't pay any attention to these girls. They're just smart-alecky kids. Let's go to your hotel."

But Sir Richard turned to Nancy. He said he remembered speaking to Mr. Drew and asked Nancy to back up her accusation. Quickly the young sleuth gave a short but full account of all her suspicions regarding Rugby and his sister. Sir Richard and his friend stared in stupefaction as Nancy concluded with the girls' imprisonment in the barn.

"Mr. Rugby—" Sir Richard started to say, then he stopped and turned to look at the suspects.

Alonzo, his sister, and the other man suddenly made a dash into the house. A moment later a rear door slammed. The girls raced after the fleeing trio but were too late to overtake them. They jumped into a car hidden among some trees and roared up the lane.

"We must go after them!" Nancy cried out, returning to the Englishmen.

"I'll drive!" said Mr. Peters. "Climb in!"

Nancy and her friends hopped into the rear and the car raced off. At the exit of the driveway they looked left and right and saw Rugby's car speeding to the north. Mr. Peters turned and sped after it.

About half a mile up the road, they came to a crossing. A police car with two officers in it was just reaching the intersection. Mr. Peters stopped and Nancy quickly told the policemen the story.

The officers said they would continue the chase. As they drove off, Nancy called, "If you find Mr. Rugby and the others, please let me know. I'm at Ivy Hall."

Nancy requested that Sir Richard drive the girls to the Patterson home. When he said he would be glad to, the young sleuth smiled. "Now I have a surprise for you."

"Haven't I had enough surprises for one day?" the Englishman asked, chuckling. "Although," he added, "I am disappointed about the window being faked."

A little dimple flickered in Nancy's cheek when she told Sir Richard that she strongly suspected the window for which he had been searching was hidden at Ivy Hall.

The man's eyebrows raised in surprise, but he said calmly, "It's worth looking into."

On reaching the mansion, Nancy introduced the Pattersons, who were astounded to hear what had happened. "What we have to show you, Sir Richard," said Sheila Patterson, "is no fake."

Nancy led him and Mr. Peters to the old library and showed them the glass behind the partition. The two men stared at it with great interest. Then Sir Richard, excited at the thought that this might be the old window which had belonged to his family, said:

Mrs. Patterson, would you permit us to take away more bricks, so that we might convince ourselves?"

"Oh, please do," Sheila replied. "I want to find out as much as you do whether this is really the old peacock window."

More tools were procured and carefully the whole group worked to uncover what was behind the bricks. Within half an hour the hind legs of a white stallion were revealed. Next came more of the horse's body, then the lower half of the knight who was riding him.

"Oh, I'm sure this is the genuine window!" Sir Richard cried out enthusiastically.

An hour later, although all the stained glass had not been uncovered, it was evident to everyone that at last Sir Richard's search had come to an end.

"And best of all," he said, "the window appears to be in good condition, even though it has been covered up. Oh, I am so grateful to you, Miss Drew."

Nancy was tingling with happiness. The strange mystery had been solved!

Sheila insisted that the weary workers relax for a while and have something to eat. With the help of Annette and Bess she prepared a delicious meal, and the group sat on the porch to enjoy it. Presently Sir Richard, looking pensive, began to tell the history of the old window.

"In 1849 my great-grandfather, Lord Henry Greystone, passed away, leaving two sons. The elder inherited not only the family home, Grey Manor, but the bulk of his father's fortune as well. The younger son, Bruce, became angry because he had not received more and left home."

Sir Richard went on to say that Bruce had come to the United States without saying good-by to anyone. At the same time the famous stained-glass window, representing an ancestor in the crusades, had also disappeared from the great entrance hall of the family home.

"The window had been there since the 1300's," the Englishman explained. "No one was ever able to trace what had become of the window after it vanished. Since my boyhood I have been fascinated by the old story and determined to find the window if it was still in existence. I had nothing to go on but a hunch that Bruce Greystone had brought the window to this country."

He smiled at Nancy and the others, saying he would not only pay the reward money to the River Heights hospital, but that he would like to buy the window from Mrs. Patterson. Sheila gave a great gulp, hardly daring to believe her good fortune.

"It's all so thrilling!" Bess sighed.

After they finished eating, Sir Richard said, "I'd like to uncover a little more of the window."

The whole group went back to the old library and started work. A few minutes later Nancy discovered a note stuck between two of the bricks. Spreading it open, she began to read the faded but still legible writing. Then, excitedly, she called the attention of the others to it and handed the note to Sir Richard. He read it aloud.

> *To the finder of this note:*
> *This stained-glass window is being covered up to preserve it during the war between the North and South. Our family has called itself Grayce since coming to this country from England in 1849. My father was Sir Henry Greystone. If none of my descendants is living when this window is found, will the finder please notify whoever is then Lord Greystone.*
> *Bruce Grayce*

Sir Richard's eyes were moist as he stared at the note. Then, in a calm voice, he said, "This is the last proof I needed."

As he paused, a car was heard driving up quickly to the house. "Maybe it's the police!" Annette said excitedly, and rushed to the hall.

She was right. An officer came to the door and asked if everyone in Ivy Hall would please step outside. In his car sat Alonzo Rugby, Mrs. Dondo, and their husky confederate.

"These three have made a full confession," the

officer reported, "but if any of you wish to question them, please go ahead."

It developed during questioning that Nancy's suspicions of Rugby and Mrs. Dondo had been correct. For some time the brother and sister had been trying to work a little racket in which they accused people of stealing letters that contained cash.

Alonzo Rugby, having heard about Sir Greystone's offer, had decided to make an imitation window. Later, he had read the *Continental* article. The sight of Nancy's peacock sketch had disturbed him, because he had thought she might have found the stained-glass window and copied the peacock on it. Later, he had changed his mind.

When Mrs. Dondo had learned through eavesdropping that Nancy was going to Virginia to hunt for the window, she had notified her brother. In order to keep the girl detective from uncovering his scheme, Rugby had first sent the fake telegram, then caused both accidents to Susan's automobile.

"What did you hope to gain by injuring us?" Nancy asked Rugby.

"I wanted to postpone your sleuthing long enough for me to complete my job," he said. "Then when you showed up at Mr. Bradshaw's, I got desperate, since I had stolen some drawings and old glass from him."

Rugby admitted wearing a mask over his face in the automobile and also when looking in the window at Susan's home. Then later he had knocked Nancy unconscious. Alarmed that she would learn his secret, he had entered the Patterson home with Mrs. Dondo, who had come from River Heights to help him.

"I wanted to make sure," he said, "that Nancy Drew had not found the real window and I had to do some hacking to satisfy myself."

Mrs. Dondo said sourly, "I searched the girls' baggage to see if there were any letters telling where it might be." She looked away. "And helped myself to a few articles."

"Well, I guess that concludes the questioning for the time being," the police officer spoke up. "Unmasking these swindlers must have been mighty exciting, Miss Drew."

Nancy agreed, but in many ways regretted that the intriguing mystery was ending and not just beginning. But soon she was to start on one of the most unusual adventures she had ever encountered, *The Haunted Showboat.*

After the prisoners were driven away, Nancy telephoned to Seven Oaks. Susan, overjoyed to hear the good news, declared, "I'll tell the Bradshaws right away!"

A little later Nancy received a call from Mark Bradshaw himself. The artist apologized profusely for his recent unfriendly attitude and thanked her for discovering the truth about Rugby.

When Nancy rejoined the group in the Ivy Hall library, everyone was staring at the exquisite stained-glass window in silent admiration.

Presently Sir Richard said dreamily, "The knight and the peacock have traveled many miles across the ocean and will have to recross it before being restored to their original home."

At that moment the telephone rang and Sheila went to answer it. When she came back, her eyes were shining happily. She stood in the center of the floor and said dramatically:

"Never again will I say that peacocks bring an actress bad luck. My agent just called—I'm to have a wonderful starring part in a new Broadway play! And, Annette, you can go to college as you've been hoping!"

"Oh, I'm so happy for us," said Annette, hugging her mother. "And we'll spend vacations at Ivy Hall!"

Nancy and Bess expressed their delight at the Pattersons' turn in fortune. George said it was great news. Then, grinning, she looked at the girl detective who had been responsible for a large part of it.

"Well, Nancy," she said, "besides solving this whole mystery and exonerating innocent people, you've even proved that peacocks are above suspicion!"